One of my favorite stories is Lynda Schor's "The Rape,"
—Doris Grumbach

It's a book you just want to read. *Appetites* is funny,
vivid, and expresses the hidden, unfreudian feelings about
everyday life and so-called love.
—Barbara Garson

She turns over the rock of female experience and reveals the
truth underneath.
—Gloria Steinem

Lynda Schor reminds me of Fellini more than any other artist
I can think of. There is no escape from feeling for a writer like
Lynda Schor. Not in distance. Not in analysis or abstraction.
Just the powerful record of experience on experience. Fortunately
for us, she has the courage, the energy, the completely original
talent to write it all down.
—Jane Lazarre

This book is recommended only to free, liberated women, who
believe that freedom and unlimited license is theirs.
—Ed Mintz, *Brooklyn Daily Bulletin*

Schor emphasizes the ridiculous, but she is a serious satirist of
the transactions between the sexes.
—Ann Barr Snitow

Few writers manage to be witty and hilarious at the same time, but Lynda Schor is—I was delighted by her stories, which encourage me to expect the unexpected: there's an astonishment on every page.
—Nora Sayre

To write about desire—of the body or the heart—requires a certain kind of fearlessness, the courage to solidify into words those deep and mysterious sensations that most of us are content merely to feel. The stories in *Appetites* are brilliant. *Appetites* pushes the boundaries of conventional good taste, but it also presses the frontiers of the short story form in important new ways . . . The ironies of everyday life become magnified. They begin to clank and rattle like ghosts chained to an unconscious past, groaning of lust and loneliness, comically exaggerated, absurd.
—Carole Rosenthal

Appetites is a collection of 12 short stories that are variously funny, bitter, surreal, and exotic. Lynda Schor writes about sex as matter-of-factly as a harried housewife trying to make food stamps stretch at the local A&P. *Appetites* is to be recommended for its honesty, its inventiveness, and above all for its meticulous attention to the details of a woman's life. Lynda Schor is the first woman writer of short stories since Grace Paley to make art from such materials.
—*Screw*

APPETITES

Lynda Schor

To Hal and Alexandra and Timothy and Zachary
In memory of Faith Sale
Thanks to Elaine Markson

H\s
HAMILTON STONE EDITIONS
P.O. Box 43, Maplewood, NJ 07040

ISBN 0-9654043-6-6

Acknowledgments: Some of these stories first appeared in the following magazines and anthologies:

Ms.: "Louise's Brownies"
Fiction: "January 28"
The Village Voice: "The Psychiatrist's Vacation"
Bitches & Other Sad Ladies: "The Rape"
Redbook: "My Death"
Last Night's Strangers: "The Horse"

TABLE OF CONTENTS

APPETITES

THE CAT

Actually it is very boring, so I sleep a lot. I lie there, hands tucked under my chest, some of my soft fur puffing over those paws so securely folded in, all my muscles relaxed, only my eyes wide, almost round, seeing all, but focusing on nothing, just closed into slits, and my body, which has always been relaxed, melts completely to a long, soft shape. Before I fall deeply asleep my nose twitches once or twice.

There's a noise; first it's a noise in my head, then I hear it as a sound and awaken. It's a squeaky twittering. I've never heard it before and I don't know why it excites me. There are louder noises, such as when the stove exploded, where I just lie there and twitch my ears, my slitlike eyes open a bit and slowly close again, until there is no opening to the inside of me; there's no part of me that isn't covered with fur; I'm secure. Just talking about how secure I feel when my orifices are closed, has put me to sleep again. And now that sound again. Before I know it, I'm on the windowsill, plastered flat against the glass, my eyes wide balls, peering into the distance, straining to see what is making my heartbeat tachycardia, and my soft, supple body is suddenly so hard, harder than I had known it could be. What on earth is it?

I don't see a thing. Yet these feelings, a sort of yearning excitement, are great but almost unbearable, and not knowing the cause is horrible, yet the whole thing is delightful.

I didn't see a thing and, left with just a strange, deep, yearning feeling, I leapt from the sill to the dark canvas sling where my roommates rest, this one shaped an especially funny way because of the way in which Bill sits, with his backside just resting on the tip of the chair, legs straight out, leaning back in a long, straight line, sometimes saying, "Judy, will you bring me my slippers?"

"Why should I? I don't ask you to bring me my slippers."

"Well, ask me. Try it, go ahead."

"Okay, Bill, will you bring me my slippers?" asks Judy.

"I would, but you don't have slippers."

"Why should I bring you your slippers like some slave or valet or something? I work too. It's not as if I were Josefa or some other cat just lying around, getting fed, her box cleaned, taken care of, loved, without doing anything in return. Nothing is expected of her—what a life."

"Because it's a woman's duty to get her husband's slippers—it always has been and it always will be."

"Ask Josefa to get you your slippers. You love her more than you love me," says Judy.

"Okay, Josefa, get me my slippers." Silence. "*Please* get me my slippers." Silence.

I just look at them. I could probably bring his slippers in my teeth if I wanted to, but why should I carry slippers to that pompous ass, stretched out in his director's chair, always directing? Let him get them himself. My look they choose to interpret as innocent stupidity.

I already know what's coming next—it's no wonder

married people get bored after a few years; they always do the same things again and again.

She says, "I wish you would just pat me and stroke me for hours like you do to Josefa, without demanding or expecting anything in return."

"Her cunt's too small," he answers smugly. "Okay, get the slippers and I'll pat you."

She runs for his slippers like a retriever, while I watch him drooling at her ass, which is sticking out of the closet while she forages for the slippers. She probably loves being stroked or tickled, as she calls it, because she falls for it every time. When she comes back with the slippers she reminds me of a dog I once saw; she seems to be panting like he was, the tip of her tongue visible between her teeth as if at any moment she might let it hang right out, leaking saliva, drooling all over Bill.

"Put them on," he says. Not content with her getting them, he has to see her bend down to the ground, in this case, a plum tweed carpet—and put them on for him; then she looks up at him, pleading for her part of the bargain. He pretends not to know what she means, and he grabs for her breast. She pleads, "Oh, come on," in a mixture of exasperation and anger, tempered with teasing. He says, "Okay." They get down on the rug. He holds up his hand like a conductor, pretends to begin gently stroking her back, in preparation for which she has lifted her shirt, and then he pinches her backside and tries to grab her cunt. She's really angry now, so he pats her to calm her, says, "Okay, okay," and sits there looking at her back as if he's thinking of something, and gives her two abstracted tickles. Her body succumbs, anger is gone; she melts closer and closer into the carpet. He's already forgetting that he's stroking her back as his other hand becomes more and more involved in turning the pages of some book.

"Hey, listen to this, Judy." (He is now lying down next to her.) "It says, 'Your cat should know his

13

name—especially if he goes outdoors. Start by addressing your cat by his name (pick a short, simple one).' "

"Like Mortimer?" At the same time as he's reading he's caressing her breasts, and—oh, I can't believe it!—she likes it, she's responding to him, she turns around and they are lying almost tight together ·and she says, "Read more."

"I'll go get the *Kamasutra* instead," he suggests.

"No, no, this is just fine, go on."

"Where am I? 'Give your cat a treat and a caress when he responds and comes.' "

"Ohhh," moans Judy.

" 'Responds and comes,' " repeats Bill, "oh, that excites me."

They are tearing off their own clothes and each other's. He begins to take off his own pants, yet before he has succeeded he's begun tugging at Judy's shirt, trying to pull it over her head. As soon as it's covering her face, but before pulling it off, he's back pulling off his own pants again. All this activity seems ridiculous to me, as I sit, my front paws crossed, moving only my eyes, observing these harmless fools. If they just went about it in a rational manner, each one undressing either himself or the other, they could be done in half the time. His underpants and slacks are tangled around one ankle and appear to be inextricable, but he doesn't seem to care, nor does he care that Judy, who is still still struggling with the shirt around her arms and head, is practically smothering, her head still covered. He grabs her down close to him and pulls off her underpants, and for some reason throws them across the room. I'm forced to move slightly, as they just miss me, but I smell their strange, funky odor as they fly by.

Then he says, "Get on the bed."

"Oh, Bill, I want you to ravish me on the rug."

"The bed's more comfortable."

"It's just that you feel ravishing me on the rug is too dissolute for your Puritan background." Meantime

14

they are already on the bed, and while she talks he presses up against her nipples, kisses her about her ears and lips—

"Listen," he whispers, still reading the book. " 'The Harness: While a collar is very decorative on the svelte body of a Siamese, a harness is more practical.' Oh, doesn't that just excite you, 'the svelte body'?" They both are caressing each other and breathing resonantly. Bill has an enormous erection, which Judy pulls on as he reads more, in a turgid voice, " 'The coat of a cat is very delicate, and a figure-eight harness is considered most practical.' " Breathing harder, choking, " 'A collar can be slipped out of—' " He gives a loud moan and places Judy's legs above her head. "Oh, I can't stand it, you read some now." Her cunt is staring straight at me now, like a mouth sideways, just looking dumb, and something sticking out a bit like her tongue when she's preoccupied. She turns her head to read. " 'Have your Siamese get used to his collar or harness by putting it on him just a few minutes . . .' "

"Oh wow." Bill, who's been diddling Judy's hairy lips with one hand, gently pulling her hair and holding up her legs with the other, can take it no longer. Those words apparently excite him so much that he quickly jumps on and inserts his enormous cock. I bounce gently with their rhythm from where I'm watching on the edge of the bed, next to their slightly pungent feet. All movement stops, Bill leans over Judy's sweaty nipple to where the book still rests, but where the pages have already flipped with their own rhythm to another page. " ' Give him a treat whenever he responds and comes, don't scold him after he's come when you've called'—isn't that great?" And I bounce faster and faster and harder, with the same nonchalant expression on my face, thinking, If they're going to use a book about cats to find out how to take care of me, they should use a book written by a cat.

15

He's lying on the now-still bed, limp, his cock long and soft like a garden hose just used, with a moist drop at the tip of it. His eyes stare moistly into the distance as if they will never open or close again. In fact, they're both lying there so dead that I begin to fear for my security, and that, besides the fact that I haven't had my evening meal, makes me hungrier than ever, so I get up and stretch by digging my front claws into the mattress right through the spread. Judy hates that, but I can't help it, it feels so good, and I start rubbing up against their legs, which are still intertwined, but hers feel stubbly and his fur is soft. As there is no response, I cry a little, a soft high cry, so high it hardly comes out until the end, but it makes them feel sorry for me, so I use it again and again. Though it looks as if he'll never speak again, Bill's the first to say, "You have to feed Josefa." His lips move, but his head and his eyes remain the same, gazing at some point in space.

"Why don't you," says Judy. "I fed him this morning."

"It's not a he it's a she, and I fed her this morning."

"I did, but anyway, I got you your slippers."

"Well, I fucked you."

"Well, you wanted to. Anyway, you act as if it's such a treat. You can take your cock and shove it up your ass."

"I would if it were longer. Let's both get up, then."

"It's too bad to have to waste manpower like this."

Bill gets up and forages for his slippers, which he won't go without even though the place is plum-tweed-carpeted from wall to wall, including the bathroom, which Judy is rushing for, something slimy running down her legs.

I'm hungry. They're starving me. When I breathe I can feel my skin against my bones. In an austere way this makes me feel good, but on the other hand, I'm too uncomfortable and I think about food all the time, but only tuna fish, and some things that Bill and Judy

16

eat. The slop that they put in my dish doesn't attract me at all. It's red and pink and ground up like cereal, with white flecks in it. That's all they want me to eat. I can't stop jumping up on the table and rubbing against their legs. When I jump on the table they become annoyed. Bill hits me, then Judy yells at Bill. She just lifts me off. "You'd think he'd learn, I'm not beating him, it's called conditioning. He can't learn if you don't punish him."

"It's not a him, it's a her."

What they can't comprehend is that it has nothing to do with learning or punishing, it's the result that counts for me, and I'm willing to try again and again. In fact, I was successful just yesterday; I got this huge chunk of real meat and fat off of Judy's plate by grabbing it sideways and being exceptionally quick. They wanted to take it away, but I kept my eyes on them and gave a deep growl until the meat was gone.

"Wow, did you see him wolf that? I didn't know cats growled." That will show them, I thought, but it hasn't changed their minds about their experiment to get me to eat that ground meat instead of that yummy tuna fish they used to give me. Apparently they read in another book that a diet of tuna fish causes liver problems. To tell you the truth, I couldn't care, I can't think in terms of long-term things. I don't want to live forever, just enjoy myself. The thing I'm beginning to realize about life is that I'm at their mercy.

Looking up, I see a white glob of flesh pressed flat and rolled over like Judy's bread dough when it's rising under that linen dishtowel that I always lift with my claws that makes Judy run into the kitchen with a rolled newspaper, the perfect punishment as described in the book, because, while it's frightening, it isn't the person's hand that's punishing, it's the newspaper. If they think I can't see who's holding it, someone's out of his mind. Then there's always a fight because you can guess whose newspaper it is that she's using, and

17

it's never yesterday's. There are slight bluish rays on the white dough, then a hand reaches up toward the toilet-paper roll, and, as the hand spins the roll, fast, ever faster, I leap and catch the stream of boutique tissue as it toboggans down, sometimes paisley, sometimes flowered. Judy, shocked out of a mesmerized state, screams. That is one of my favorite games. I do it all the time. I lie low and quiet in wait. Considering how often I do it, one would think they'd be prepared, but I always surprise them.

When I'm lying low I'm crouched down, my body is tense, my head tucked in, ears back, and only my eyes wide, looking up as if they would crawl up my head any minute. I watch their flesh hang over the toilet seat, waiting for the hand to move, her ass hanging over the edges, his sitting neatly on—I can't tell which I prefer. I enjoy her scream, whereas Bill tends to hit out when surprised, and though it's more exciting, I've actually been hit more than once.

One day I'm lying flat against the outside of the bathtub, trying to keep cool, and I hear those strange noises again. The ones that excite me. I twitch my ears without moving. The sounds again. Besides a weird, sensuous feeling, a surge of adrenaline causes me to spring up and bound over to the window. The source of the sound is something flying. The twittering sound plus the surging motion of the creature excites me. I step out tentatively on the sill, totally involved in the flying movements, my body moves tensely, slightly, my eyes following every subtle curve and swoop. I feel as if I'm flying with the animal. I don't know what I'm waiting for, until the animal perches on a vent pipe on the terrace. All of a sudden I feel myself pounce. I'm on the vent pipe, trying to get a hold with my claws on the sloped top. I hear my nails scratching the metal as I scramble ludicrously, trying to get hold. The bird has long since flown, seems to be watching me, flying to and fro above me, chirping away as I fall clumsily to

18

once a week to make sure it's still in place. Foam is next, but, like the condom, we don't recommend it as a permanent method of contraception. That's all, ladies, I'll take you downstairs now, where you and the doctor can discuss what method is best for you. Don't forget your pants," she said as she closed the door behind her.

Downstairs again. Finally the doctor called me into a small room, where I was instructed to get onto the usual table. "When was the last time you had intercourse, Mrs. Rosenzweig?" she asked, peering at my cunt. There was a short pause as we both waited for it to answer.

Then I said, "Oh, last night of course. We would have this morning, too, only my husband was late for work." I blushed.

"And what method of contraception did you use?"

"Jelly. Number five," I answered, referring to the little gray booklet. I would have liked to say that it was something else that I'd used, but I was afraid that she was testing my honesty, since I had already said I used jelly to the lady who filled out my chart.

"Well, you realize that we don't recommend jelly," she said. "I'll have a look at you and then we'll see. I understand you haven't menstruated since the birth of your baby?"

"Yes, I'm nursing him," I said.

She jammed her white-gloved middle finger up my poor, worn-out vagina with vigor. She fiddled around a bit, pressing in my abdomen with her other hand. She said, "Wait a minute," and went out, without removing her glove. She brought two other women back with her, which made the small room very crowded. They've found out and are going to punish me, I thought. My knees involuntarily closed and were pulled apart by one of the nurses.

"Look," she said, as they all peered under the sheet. "Most of the hymen's still attached. She had a virgin birth." "Excellent stitching job . . . No, I don't believe

73

it, no episiotomy!" She exclaimed in wonder. "How did you do that?" she asked. "That's marvelous!"

"Natural childbirth," I said.

Then she told me that, in all good conscience and in order to be perfectly cautious, she couldn't insert an IUD because the cervix was slightly enlarged and fairly soft, not as firm as it should be. She looked at me with her cold eyes. "I'm sorry, Mrs. Rubinstein, I just cannot. I'll give you pills, but they'll probably dry up your milk."

"No thanks, then," I said.

When she smiled apologetically I noticed the lipstick smears on her teeth, blurred by tears balanced between my lids. I got off the table and attempted to pull down my skirt with dignity. Somewhere or other I had lost my pants. At the desk I was given a bill for twenty dollars and seventy-five cents.

"But I didn't get anything," I screamed, tears streaming down. All the women were watching me as in a theater, on their bridge chairs. "What shall I pay for?"

"Well, the examination alone is ten dollars and seventy-five cents," the secretary said.

"But I didn't ask for the examination," I said.

"But it was given."

"I only have seventy-five cents," I said. "You'll have to bill me." The doctor, hearing my screaming, came out of the room to watch me cry. Outside, I castigated myself for giving them seventy-five cents, but I was paying for my guilt.

That night my friend, who was eleven but had breasts larger than my mother's, took me to visit a neighbor of hers who loved babies but couldn't have any, so she had a dog instead. Our plan was to ask her whether she would like to buy the baby from me after it was born. She'd only have to give me a small deposit now, in order to guarantee the contract. It was not the best plan,

74

but better than nothing. We rang her bell, standing close together.

"Who is it?"

"Andrea."

"Andrea who? I don't know any Andrea."

"Andrea Greenhood, your neighbor from upstairs." She stood on tiptoe in order to be more visible through the peephole.

"You have to be careful nowadays," she said. She opened the door but didn't let us in. "What is it?" No one answered. "How is your mother?"

"Fine, thanks. Could we speak to you for a moment?"

"You mean, could you speak *with* me."

"Yes, could we speak with you for a minute?"

"You mean for a moment."

I thought, God, what an awful mother she'd be, but in my degree of desperation it wouldn't have occurred to me to refuse her my child—or, for that matter, I wouldn't have refused anyone, even crazy old Mrs. Firestone upstairs, if she offered to take it and keep quiet. As she stood in the doorway I looked straight through the rollers over which her bleached hair was tightly wrapped to the room beyond, like looking through telescopes. She gave us milk and Chipareenos at her Formica dinette, while a black, nondescript dog of medium size gazed at us cheerfully and groggily, with his pinkish tongue lolling out, relaxed. Then he gave a smile and a yawn, with his ears back.

"Ohhhh, hi, sweetheart, you're up." Mrs. Duvernoy picked up the sleepy dog, held him in her arms like a baby, and sat down at the table. The dog's tiny tongue was out and vibrated like a machine.

"Did you ever see such a sweet baby?" she asked us.

"He's nice," I said. "How old is he?" which is a question I always reserve for discussing dogs, because I think dogs are disgusting and stupid, with their forever lapping all over people, and waiting to eat garbage, chicken bones, and all kinds of things bad for them as

75

soon as they're left to their own devices, including feces.

"Isn't he sweet," she asked no one, as the dog nibbled at her hand and fingers. "It's teething, isn't it, but such a good little boy. Already paper-trained." That last remark wasn't very encouraging. Perhaps Mrs. Duvernoy had wanted a baby but was willing at this point to become used to the simpler needs of a dog.

Andrea said, "Since you have always professed a love for children and have always said you wished you had some, my friend would like to know whether you'd like to buy one—at a very low rate." Mrs. Duvernoy was smiling and patting her dog, who relaxed on her lap, freckled belly upright, a single drop of liquid on his pubic hair.

"How much would you charge?" she asked.

"We decided on twenty-four dollars, the price of Manhattan Island—plus tax, of course. It's going to be a boy, and our only request is that you call it Jesus, after the father's wishes."

"Are you serious?" she asked. "In the first place, Mr. Duvernoy and I have discussed it and we've decided that if it can't be one of our own, we don't want any. If it's not your own flesh and blood you never know what you're getting. Whose baby is it? Someone you know?"

"Yes," I said, deciding that, since it would be impossible to sway her, I wouldn't let her know it was mine.

"How could the woman be so callous as to want to sell her own child, her own flesh and blood, begot in her own body, a human baby. How could she do it after feeling the life in her body, her own child, moving and turning within . . ." Mrs. Duvernoy was already weeping as she spoke, and tears were streaming through her powder. I was in tears myself but didn't want to show it. All that stuff about the baby moving in your body was really beginning to get at me, and I wanted

76

to leave before Mrs. Duvernoy's rollers started to fall to the inlaid linoleum.

"You tell your friend that she's downright inhuman, absolutely inhuman. That there could be inhuman humans is totally inhuman. Those are the inhuman humans that cause all the crime." We heard her fitting the bar of the Fox lock as we boarded the elevator.

Andrea had another idea. She said she'd heard that it was possible to obtain an abortion if I could be proven mentally unfit to care for a baby. We composed a letter to St. Vincent's Hospital. If I could convince the doctor to write a note stating that I was ill (crazy), I could tell my mother I was sleeping over a friend's house, and get an abortion. We wrote:

Dear Sir:

I am ten years old and in desperate trouble, which I can't cope with. I can't speak to anybody, I can't sleep, I'm considering becoming a drug addict, I have violent depressions, and if I can't see a psychiatrist soon I will probably commit suicide. I can't even study. Please make an appointment for me soon.

Thank you.

Yours truly,
Michele Levy.

Three days later I received a letter giving me an appointment to be interviewed by a Michael Price. I went to the hospital and showed someone my letter. I was told not to go anywhere, that the doctor would be out to get me. I sat down and instead of trying to pretend that I was nutty, I found myself trying to pretend that I was supersane. My hands were shaking as they reached over a large pseudo-coffee-table for the *Catholic Digest*. I was developing a twitch near my eye and one in my upper lip. I considered it a bad omen that there was a large crucifix on the wall, the only ornament besides a clock and a very El Greco-type painting of some trustee. I sat with the magazine in my lap, fascinated by the crucifix. Jesus Christ hung there, droplets of blood pouring from his head where he wore his crown of thorns, his hands, his heart, and his ankles. And yet he was smiling. That is probably why this particular one was in a psychiatric clinic. Soon a nun came out to greet me. At first I thought it was a mistake, but she introduced herself as Sister Michael Price. I didn't think the fact that she had a mustache was enough justification for her to take the name of Michael.

"I'm just going to interview you," she said. "Then you'll get an appointment with an appropriate doctor." She put a large sheet of paper into her typewriter. The top of the typewriter hid her face to just above her mustache. It occurred to me that she was one of God's wives. She had actually married him in a ceremony. Why couldn't he have given her his child? Now I was involved in adultery too.

"How old are you?" she asked.

"Ten."

"Do you take drugs?"

"No."

"Have you ever had sexual relations?"

"Once."

"With a man?"

"Yes. Sort of."

"Have you ever had a homosexual experience?"

"No, but I have some problems with dogs."

She looked up. "Dogs?"

"They're always trying to sniff me."

"What do you mean 'sniff you'?"

"Sniff me, that's all," I said, closing the subject.

"How do you feel about that?" asked Sister Michael.

"I hate it—it embarrasses me, it's so primitive, and all the time I have to pretend that it's not happening."

She typed on her notes for a while, then asked, "Why are you here?"

"Because I'm pregnant and I'm not well. I'm sure

78

I'll do something harmful to the baby—I'm not capable of caring for it."

"Do you have a mother? Why don't you tell your mother? Perhaps once you do that all will be okay. Maybe you'll see how pleased she'll be to help you."

"I can't tell my mother, she's not strong and can't take any trouble. I always have to protect her from trouble. She has a very insulated life and I'm afraid she might crack. And then she might yell and hit me, and I can't stand that."

I began to cry. I was so totally exhausted from all these examinations and interviews, all this fiddling with my mind and body, to no avail. I was really terrified. All this time I was, somehow, still schmucky enough to believe that somehow, when it really got rough, He would come, like Superman, out of the sky and rescue me. Now, for the first time, all of me realized that no one was going to help. I wept in front of Sister Michael Price with real despair, and she said, "Okay, that's all for today, Miss Levy, we'll notify you when we've set up an appointment."

I searched my mother's sewing drawer for her knitting needles, which I was unsuccessful in finding. Would I be frustrated at every turn? I decided to substitute an OO crochet hook, which I stuck into my heavy white sock. I went into the bathroom, and sure enough, it took me a long time to find the hole.

"Oh my god." Mrs. Levy saw the blood dripping through the mattress onto a carpet that shows no dirt. She became pale and thought she would faint. She didn't dare to go closer for fear of what she would find. She called Isobel, who didn't want to inspect the scene more closely either but who managed to call an ambulance.

"*Oi vey*, it's suicide," said Mrs. Levy. She picked up a letter from the maple dresser. It read:

79

Dear Dr. S——,

I am very ill and it is most important that I see you for medical help. I have been ill for two months now and soon it will be too late. Please write and tell me if I can have an appointment.

Yours truly,
Michele Levy

On the reverse side of the letter, in another handwriting, it said:

I regret to inform you that the doctor has been in jail for the past three months. I can recommend Dr. P—— of Baltimore. The fee will be four hundred and seventy-five dollars.

"She was sick, she's sick and she never told anybody, oh god." She was standing there like a ninny when the men from the ambulance rang the bell, but Isobel was already at the window because she heard the sickening thud of the stretcher being removed, and she ran to open the door. When she hurried the drivers into the room they found that my mother had fainted, so they lifted us both onto the stretcher, making unseemly cracks about my mother's weight.

When my mother awoke at the hospital she felt much better because she'd been given a sedative. There was a Social Service lady by her side, waiting to interview her.

"My daughter, she's sick—*oi vey*," my mother told the lady immediately, showing her the letter she had found, which was so crumpled and sweaty that there was no more ink on it.

"Your daughter is pregnant, Mrs. Levy."

"Oh no, it couldn't be, she's just ill. Here, read this letter." And she tried again to hand the woman the letter, which looked like a large spitball.

"This is the crochet hook that we removed from your daughter's vagina."

80

"So there was a crochet hook up there, what does that prove?"

"Look, Mrs. Levy, your daughter's in labor right now."

"Maybe it's not my daughter; she was on my daughter's bed, but I didn't look at her face."

"We need some data. Will you please try and be cooperative? Your daughter's name?"

"Michele Levy."

"Her age?"

"Ten."

"Married or unmarried?"

"Oh, married . . . no, divorced . . . divorced."

"Her first child?"

"Yes."

"Religion?"

"Jewish."

"What is your income, Mrs. Levy?"

"I don't know. My husband's a retired postal worker; we have no money for this sort of thing. Listen, I'm sure I can speak for my child: she wouldn't want that baby, and I can't take care of it. Can't it just be gotten rid of quietly? I mean, she is aborting, isn't she?"

"We're doing all that's possible to save the baby, Mrs. Levy. It's the hospital policy. We have a psychiatric counselor with Michele right now in the labor room, and if it becomes incumbent upon us to allow the life of the fetus to terminate, upon his recommendation and that of a body of doctors and priests, who will meet in a few moments to consult on the matter and then vote, we shall see what the outcome will be. In the meantime have faith that the best possible course will be decided for your child."

Because of a shot they gave me in the backside I was very groggy and repeatedly fell asleep, only to be awakened by the most incredible pain or pressure which began somewhere in my abdomen, remaining there for only a second, then rapidly spread to my whole body, pushing down on my legs until I thought they would fall off, while my torso became a tight swollen ball. I could do nothing but scream and thrash. Someone came in and pulled up the sides of my bed, and as if that clang of metal were a signal, a man came in and sat down beside the bed.

"I'm a psychiatrist. I want to help you." I had no desire to stop screaming just because he was there. He seemed totally at ease.

"If you want to help me, do something about this pain," I croaked. For a few moments I actually believed that he would, or could, but that illusion didn't last long. He just sat there silently for a while.

"Why are you resisting me?" he asked.

"What do you mean?" I panted groggily.

"Perhaps you want to tell me what's wrong. You almost killed yourself, you know."

"That's nothing compared to what's happening to me now!" I screamed. "Help, here comes another one!" The psychiatrist was beginning to shuffle in his seat, his frog face expressing impatience with my pain, which was interrupting us every few moments.

"You're very young," he said. "Were you raped?"

"Yes," I said.

"Are you lying?"

"Yes. If you want to know the truth, God came to me one night, after being introduced by the Holy Ghost. He laid me, and I became pregnant, and I didn't even really like him—the whole thing was so nothing."

"I can see that you aren't going to cooperate," he said, looking nervously about him.

"What do you mean—"

"You want me to believe that you're insane so that I'll recommend an abortion for you, but I see through that. It's childish of you to think that I might not. If you'd been seeing a psychiatrist before it would be different, but now you're trying to use me in order to effect something that you don't-know the magnitude of. I can't allow you to do that."

82

"Some psychiatrist," I said. "If I don't say what you want, or expect, then what I do say has no validity to you." Actually, this conversation might have been depressing, but I was really out of it, either totally groggy or in incredible pain. It just didn't seem important. I had no idea why anyone was discussing the subject of abortion, nor did I care. I was so sure that what was happening to me now was an abortion, and that if I lived through it I would just go home. Two or three doctors or nurses threw me onto a narrow table, which they wheeled into another room. One put white leggings on me while another strapped my wrists to two metal things, and as I flapped my hands from them like trapped pigeons, someone put a mask over my face and told me to breathe in, which I did gratefully, gasping ungracefully. I longed for oblivion.

As soon as my eyes opened I was admonished not to move, then my mother, aware somehow that I was awake, lunged hopefully in my direction.
"Are you okay? How do you feel? How could you do this to me."
When I lifted my head to speak to her I saw a glass or plastic globe with fluid in it, and swimming about, attached to a long, slithery rope, was a tiny fetus, with a large head and almost nonexistent limbs, and closed protruding eyes on the sides of its head.
"Don't move," I was told again.
"What's that?" I asked.
"That's your baby," the nurse said. "Isn't she cute? It's a girl. We saved her. Bet you didn't think we could. Practically the whole hospital was mobilized. That's an artificial uterus," she said, pointing to the plastic globe, "but the baby is still attached to the placenta, which is still in your body. So you'll have to lie still for just a few more months and then you'll be able to take her home. If you don't lie still you'll have to be strapped down."

83

"Jesus Christ," I screamed, "this is just like the Middle Ages!"

"You'll have to be more quiet," said the nurse. "What do you want to name her?"

"Jesus," I said.

"Well?"

"Jesus."

"Oh, that's what you want to name her? I thought you were still cursing."

"My daughter doesn't curse," said mother, her jowls swinging. Then she screamed, "Jesus, that's not a girl's name, and besides it's not a Jewish name." She began to cry again, her tiny red lashless eyes filling with fluid.

"Well, you can tell everyone that her name's Judy."

"Will it really be Judy?"

"No, Jesus."

"Oh, what am I going to do? I can't tell anyone about the baby. You'd better think of something, since it's your fault."

"Okay, mother, you go home and I'll think of something." I watched the fetus swim around for a while, then I screamed, "It's a girl!" And I laughed so hard that someone came in and gave me a shot.

If you think it was hard for me to lie there so long, you're wrong. I was so totally worn out, and perhaps the fact that the fetus was still attached to me drained my energy, but I felt weak and enjoyed it. I felt totally sheltered. I didn't have to deal with any problems; it was a time of reprieve. My mother and sister came to visit me less and less because they became accustomed to my being there and had commitments at home. This was very lovely for me because it allowed me to indulge in my favorite fantasy, and that was planning how I would get rid of that fetus in the globe. Thinking about it gave me shivers, like when I'd stolen a balloon from Woolworth's. At first I just let the thought excite me, before I tried to turn it into a real plan. It was a diaphanous dream, enveloping me in security, but the

84

most concrete desire I had had so far in my life, with no one but me to execute it. The feeling that I would really do it flipped me. I allowed many different plans, all intermixed, to enter me like various nightmares, where the parts are not consecutive. They frightened and pleased me at the same time. During the day someone would probably be in in time to save it, and at night my arms and legs were strapped to prevent any movement that might disengage the cord from the placenta, or the placenta from me. I watched the fetus a lot. It swam quite a bit and reminded me of a goldfish I once had that developed a white spot on its side which grew larger until the fish couldn't balance anymore, and swam on its side. When it died my mother flushed it down the toilet.

When I decided to do it, it was a bright day, and a ray of murky light reflected off the globe my baby swam in. I got up very cautiously, holding the umbilical cord over my wrist as if it were the sash of my bathrobe, trying to avoid all strain, not knowing what would happen to me or the placenta when I got up. It was possible that it might fall out and I would faint from weakness and bleed to death. That would be one solution to the problem, but it wasn't my favorite one. I'd decided not to die just from spite, because here were all these people telling me what to do, and they were all so sweet while I was lying there vegetating, feeding that parasite.

The fact that I could see it from up close didn't make me change my mind about killing the ugly old thing. I felt a swish, as if a huge amount of liquid had been suddenly expelled from my vagina. Apparently that's all it was, because the placenta still seemed to be within me, from what I could tell by the whereabouts of one end of the cord. The glass (or plastic) of the dome was very nearly unbreakable, though I applied my hairbrush first, my comb, and then my water pitcher. It finally split at a neat, invisible seam, while the contents slid to the floor in a lubricated torrent.

85

The fetus in no way thwarted my decision by showing any signs of life other than a heartbeat so speedy that it was almost a twitch. It looked more like a dead frog that had faded in the sun than anything human. I almost had to saw the cord, which was goopy, with my nail scissors and nail file, and some other articles of beauty which my mother was considerate enough to bring to keep up my morale while I was incubating my young. I picked it up with one of those wipes that they always leave on hospital tables, and took it to my little private bath, which so far I had been unable to use, and was just about to flush the toilet—Who knows how many babies are left to grow up in the sewers of America? I thought—when the nurse came in.

"What are you doing?"

"I just got up to go to the bathroom," I said, and fainted.

When I awoke I had to close my eyes again immediately. I opened them more carefully the next time, and saw that there were huge spotlights on and my little room was crowded with people. It seemed to be about two hundred degrees Fahrenheit, but I didn't dare touch my blanket, because my room looked like a TV studio. Someone was just about to make a speech. Did I dare? Yes. I looked over at the bubble, the goldfish bowl, the imitation uterus, and sure enough they had it patched up with a rubber hose taped to its navel, and the other end presumably taped to my placenta, which was probably taped to my uterus.

"I don't know how many of us are aware that in many homes the parents—or more usually, one parent —beat either one or more—usually one—of their children, senseless, until they have concussions, broken bones, et cetera, until the last beating, which is too much for the poor child and it is finally brought into the hospital just in time to die. Dr. Curran, of Our Lady of Most Precious Blood, working in conjunction with Dr. Fitzpatrick of Our Lady Perpetual Martyr Hospitals, both heads of the pediatric departments, developing their reputations in the field of discovering parents who beat their children, will speak to you now."

"The reason I'm speaking to you tonight, ladies and gentlemen, is because something happened here, right here at this hospital, which I am concerned with. A young mother, ten years old, tried to flush her baby down the toilet after an unsuccessful attempt at self-induced abortion. Grim. But this isn't one case. The statistics are grim . . . grim. Some of the children who come to the emergency room are nearly dead, and when they are X-rayed it's discovered that many of their small bones have been broken and healed over and over again. We must prosecute these parents instead of allowing the children to go home with them again and again. We must put these children in foster homes, but most of all we must have more stringent punishments for these types of crimes. Luckily, we saved the life of this baby time and time again." The camera moves in toward the baby in the globe. "But should this mother go unpunished? No. Punishment is the answer. The young lady's trial will come up when she and the child are released from the hospital. Now Dr. Joyce Caruthers, a psychologist, will explain why some parents beat their children."

My mother came to visit me on Tuesdays, after her Weight Watchers meeting. She plainly dreaded the day I would come home with the baby.

"Couldn't we just give her up for adoption?"

"Certainly, mother," I said, "whatever you say. I can't think about it anymore."

She spoke to the head nurse about it, who said that if I gave up the child it would be worse for me at my trial—in fact, I'd probably be sent right to a reformatory—whereas if I kept the child I'd probably just be put on probation. I read a magazine while mother questioned the nurse about reformatories. Later she told me that the food in reformatories wasn't that bad.

I had one more plan: I'd return this baby to God by leaving her in front of a church. I'd be rid of her and perhaps she'd have a good life. Perhaps they'd recognize the holy genes in her.

The baby was about the size of a quail, only thinner, when they injected me with something which caused a few pains and expelled the afterbirth, which looked like my kidney, but they assured me it wasn't. They put the baby in an incubator. When I saw her she had wires in her head, like a wreath, to ascertain whether she had incurred any brain damage. It was easy for me to get her out; I felt so much better now. I just got dressed and walked down the stairs, carrying her like a doll, all the wires still sticking out of her head. She was wrapped in my towel and washcloth, fresh from Consolidated Laundry, and tears were streaming down my eyes because she was warm and soft like a puppy that you aren't allowed to keep. In fact, after all those lonely months in the hospital, holding that warm body was a most wonderful feeling. The church steps were concrete, and I had misgivings about placing her on them, as I had no basket, or even shoebox, to put her in. I'd have liked to write a note saying, "Her name is Jesus." The door I was going to put her in front of was a magnificent heavy door with a brass doorknob emerging from a sculpted brass cross with a beautiful filigree of people and flowers all over it. I was hung up digging the cross when the door opened and the baby, which I held in front of me, was impaled on the knob. It hung there sadly, with the large cross behind it, and the wires still all around her head. A priest stood in the doorway and stared at her for a moment, as I did.

"You killed it," he said softly.

"No, you killed her!" I screamed. He tried to grab me but I ran into the basement, down a stairway in the

88

only direction open to me, and he followed. He was gaining on me and I was in a frenzy, a panic. I found myself in some kind of church bazaar which luckily was very crowded, but the priest was gaining on me. I saw a cashier and a stairway. I stole a scarf on my way out and kept running.

LOUISE'S BROWNIES

I'm lying on the large bed. The clean sheets feel so cool. I have nothing on but my Lamston's bikinis, which used to be white, but are brownish gray because I can never learn how to do the laundry like on TV, plus my socks, which come up to the middle of my calves and are bright green with orange apples woven in. I'm staring through the glass door, and across the long expanse of terrace, at the blue beaded lights of the Queensboro Bridge. A door opens near the bed, lighting the dim room for a moment, revealing a full-length mirror in which is reflected the sparkling, large space of Alan's private bathroom. The fluorescent bathroom light shooting sparks of whiteness off the tile and enamel fixtures is suddenly obscured by Alan's long body, which is in the doorway for a moment, dark, with all the light behind it, then light, as he shuts the door behind him. We lie next to each other on the red-white-and-blue percale sheets that his mother bought for him with her discount at B. Altman. I take a glass of wine off the nighttable, sit up higher, and sip it. It's dry and cold, filled with reflections from the only lamp that's lit, which move around inside the glass as I shake it gently around to watch the different shades of soft gold, bright yellow, and pale maize. Alan, sitting on the edge of the bed, dips his hand into a dish of hard, smooth, beige cookies.

"Have one of these gingerbread cookies Louise baked." He picks up his wineglass after rubbing his fingers together in a circular motion against each other to rid them of a pale, clinging powder from the cookies. "Is the wine good?"

"It's yummy."

He looks down at my body, which is again reclining. The only thing he's wearing are his tortoise-shell eyeglasses. I can see his dimple deepen above the edge of his black beard.

"You're a funny girl. You sure have funny socks," he says, referring to my magnificent kelly-green foot coverings.

"I don't think these are funny socks at all. I think yours are funny, those black, sleazy, short Jewish socks."

"Well, I got them on sale on Delancey Street."

"Then they really are Jewish socks."

He smiles. I take his set of Flair pens from his desk. A whole box of them, beautiful colors. I pick out magenta first and begin to draw a tiny flower on his upper thigh as he lies there smiling, content.

Later, when I waken and turn on the lamp, I find that the tattoo I had painted on Alan has transferred its image into three blurred flowers near the indentation at the top of my thigh. Alan wakes. I can see the whole city through the terrace doors, yet, perhaps because the door is closed, there is an irrelevant silence, unless it is the hour. We dress in silence too, my teeth clenched with the sensation of cold I feel when looking outside. I'm searching all the underedges of the bed for my socks and underpants, strewn in total disregard for where they would land, and my shirt and slacks, which were, in contrast, placed neatly over a chair. I open the bedroom door and descend the small flight of cold hardwood stairs, carrying my platform shoes so

91

that I won't wake his three children, who're asleep in the downstairs bedrooms. Alan is still upstairs in his bathroom and I use one of the children's bathrooms, where, in this overabundance of baths, one shower is completely preempted by four enormous turtles, bits of chopped-meat fat still lurking about the edges of their water.

I'm standing by the large window next to the couch while Alan ties the shoelaces of his gray Hush Puppies. It's dark except for the faraway light in the kitchen. I can see a man and woman in robes, sitting at a table, through the window of the high-rise across the street. Aside from that, everything is dark. Looking across the downstairs terrace, I can see a small portion of the East River, roaring and tumbling, wild and cold. For a moment I get a feeling of space and adventure, watching the turbulence, then suddenly I shiver deeply with perception again, of the cold outside, which has nothing to do with the warmth inside.

I walk to the large hall closet, where Alan is taking out my coat. I put out my hand to take it, when suddenly as usual, he opens it like a matador with a cape, flipping it swiftly in such a way that suddenly facing me is the torn, two-tone, faded purplish-mauve lining (perhaps once worn by Joan Crawford), and I half turn to accept the coat with one shoulder, as it always makes me feel strange to have someone put on my coat for me. Alan puts three crumpled dollars into my hand for the taxi. Two seventy-five, plus tip. I always add another quarter or two to the driver's tip.

I say, "Is that all I was worth?" He smiles a rubber-band smile as if, not sure of my joke, it could snap back at any moment to his usual expression.

On the way out the door he asks, "Want some brownies Louise baked?"

In the lobby the doorman is sleeping. I hate going out in the middle of the night in the middle of winter, but I can't stay over because my kids are home in my own apartment. I'm frozen, huddled into my antique fur coat, given to me by Irene because, luckily, her arms are too long for it. Alan hails a cab. I sit huddled inside, waiting for some warmth to pervade my body again, and my smile is frozen at Alan's tentative good-night smile, which disappears into York Avenue, and the faint, pale brown of his new sheepskin coat that his mother got with her discount at B. Altman.

Timothy is in the corner of his room, puffed up to twice his fatness and red as a beet. He's plastered against the wall, his arm raised, holding his waterproof vinyl cowboy boot. He wants to throw it. Zachary is plastered to my knees and beginning to twine around them like a snake, making it impossible for me to move farther into the room, which is only seven feet wide anyway, so, being in the doorway, I'm only a few feet from Timothy against the wall.

"Don't throw that boot!" I shout. "What happened?"

"Gggggggghhhhaaaoooouuuuugggggeeeeemmmmeeee."

"I can't understand one word if you talk while you're crying. Stop crying and calm down and tell me."

"Zachary and I were playing, Lynda, then hesssaalll mmmmvmvmv aaaahhhhhhhhhhhh."

"What? I didn't hear the rest because you were crying again. Start over." I'm holding him gently around his legs, but he still doesn't put down the boot. Zachary is under the wooden desk.

"Zachary gave me his GI Joe for this box of Chiclets, Lynda, so I gave him the whistle, Lynda, plus the box of Chiclets for the GI Joe, and then I said he should give me something else, Lynda, because I gave him something else, so he gave me the jeep too, Lynda, and now he wants them back, Lynda."

"But you have to admit that it isn't a fair trade, Timothy. You're taking advantage of him."

"But last year, Lynda, you bought him that trailer, and you only bought me that set of tiny men for my birthday."

93

"That's because you got the bike before your birthday."

"Well, it's not fair, Lynda. I'm not giving back his GI Joe, Lynda."

I can see that with all these references and cross references to the past, no logical answer will ever suffice. I could always threaten never to buy them anything again, but I know I won't stick to it. I remind Timothy of our blanket solution: "I thought I told you never to trade with him again because he's younger and always wants to trade back. If you insist on trading with him, then do it for a while, and when he wants to trade back, do it."

Alexandra is swinging from the edge of the sleeping loft with all the agility of a spider monkey. She says, "Timo takes advantage of Zachary. He trades him all this junk for good stuff." I don't feel like reminding her about the little piece of wool that she just swapped Zach for his new looseleaf notebook with the new paper in it. Accidentally her foot, still wearing the boot with the studs and ecology signs on it that her father got for her on Twelfth Street and Avenue B but which I gave him the money for, hits Timothy in the mouth. He whacks her with his cowboy boot, screaming and crying, Alex shouting, "It was an accident, it was an accident, it was an accident!"

"It was not, Alex. You hit me with your shoe, you kicked me in the mouth, Alex."

"Mommmmmmyy," Alex is screaming, still hanging off the sleeping loft by one hand, trying to protect herself with the other from the blows of the heavy vinyl boot. The doorbell rings. Oh god, is it eight o'clock already? I wonder how I can go out and leave them in this condition. I unlock the door. It's Alan, his smile towering there in the dim light of the dusty hallway, the filthy gray marble stairs and ocher lead-poison paint glowing sickeningly in the special light of the low-wattage bulbs, a unique quality of most of the buildings I've lived in, behind him.

94

"Hi," he says, his smile broadening. As I open the door, the bookshelf hiding the hole over the doorway falls from the wall, injuring no one—*Pale Fire* and *24 One-Act Plays*, and others, crashing together like opposing waves at the seashore.

"Hi," I say, extricating myself from a hello kiss to run back into the room where part of me wishes the kids to fight it out by themselves and part wants to get it all straightened out immediately so that I can leave, feeling the sensation of some kind of order. Now, down from the loft, Alex is actively beating Timothy.

"Well, he hit me with the shoe."

"But you started."

"But it was an accident, and he really hit me."

Timothy is screaming now. Zach is still under the desk, relieved that the focus is off him. He's holding his GI Joe, which he's retrieved, and trying to get Timothy to take it, perhaps to pacify him so that he ceases that incredible screaming. Alan is standing there half watching through the large doorway, framed in large, heavy, yellow vinyl curtains, as if we're in a play which he's not part of. He's partly mesmerized by the steady drip emanating from the hole in the ceiling over the radiator where the damp beams are exposed, some wet plaster suppurating around the opening like the edges of a wound, drops of water dripping through and around the plants, making soft plops on the clothes from three loads of laundry that's drying on the radiator because my line fell down yesterday with all the clothes on it, which had to be rewashed, each droplet on the clothes surrounded by a fine, ragged white outline of plaster dust.

I tell Alex to get out of the room and practice her guitar. Long, sleepy wails are still emanating from Timothy's mouth; his pink, wet face looks like a Spaulding that's fallen into a puddle. I look at Alan. He looks at me deeply and says, "Hi," again, his eyes trying to extract a happy hello for himself as one extracts a suitcase of valuables from an earthquake. I smile inappropriately like a schizophrenic. I'm almost ready to go. Alex reappears in the front room, which is two feet from her room, and where there are fallen books all over the floor. Alan is waiting for me on the studio couch, which is really a high-riser covered with an Indian spread.

"You just went out last night," says Alex. "You can't go out tonight. You always go out."

"It's almost bedtime anyway. Why do I have to sit here and keep you company while you sleep? Besides, you went to Emily's last weekend, why can't I go out too?"

"But-you just went out. You go out every night."

"No, I don't. I did go out a lot this week, but so what? Two nights are for school."

"You can't go out."

"Two years ago my kids were just like that," says Alan. He makes me feel better, saying it isn't just me. I end up promising not to go out quite so much, which isn't my idea of a good solution.

"This term's almost over. Then I won't be out so much," I say. They each kiss me many times, each not wanting the other to have more kisses, in a combination ritualistic, manipulative goodbye, forcing me, as if in a game, to repeat again and again a gesture that becomes more and more meaningless, as a way of venting their anger at my leaving, and I kiss them again, feeling more and more spiteful, until I shout, "Enough!" Somehow I feel manipulated into leaving with a sour parting instead of a neat, pleasant one, the way I'd like. I hear the click of the lock behind me as we descend the stairs, my platform shoes making a familiar clunking noise on the worn, dirty, gray stone steps of the hallway.

When we get back I run in to check the kids, with my usual sense of doom, but they're all asleep on their own loft beds; there's order, aside from an enormous mess of papers and orange peels, their semidried deep orange against the turquoise of my Deluxe Rya and the tiny orange pits nestling in the extra-long fibers. I go to the bathroom, first wiping the plaster and the water off the seat from the leak in the ceiling, which has been fixed six times and is leaking again, so no one bothers to plaster the hole again. I often imagine that the people who live in the apartment above can peer through into my bathroom and watch me in there, but I know that's not true. All I can see are pipes. The light isn't working. It probably just needs a bulb, but it can't be reached without a ladder, even by me standing on the edge of the high old-fashioned bathtub, as the ceilings are eleven feet high, even though the bathroom is three feet by four feet. By the time I come out of the bathroom Alan's already undressed, an unsubtle nonco-quettish quality of speed inherent in the expression of his desire. He's standing beside a pile of his clothes, his penis beckoning to me with a slightly upturned angle, erect already, even though I hadn't been in the room at all until that moment. We kiss, and then I shut the door to Alex's room, as it's very close to mine and mine doesn't have a door that shuts, as it's also the living room and is connected with the kitchen and a small dining room by enormous doorways that are almost as large as the rooms themselves. By the time I'm finished, which is about two seconds, Alan is gone. Then I see his face peering down at me from the edge of my sleeping loft, which was built by my husband before we separated. I smile.

"You sure are horny for a professor." I take off my slacks and socks, which are magenta with an orange ice-cream cone woven in on the sides, and climb the ladder to the loft bed with my shirt on. Lately it bothers me the way men look at me when I'm completely naked. Not the way you look at a person. Alan is helping me remove my shirt when I notice a cockroach walking slowly along the molding ten feet above the ground, but directly above my head. I pick up my white diaphragm case and smash it. Alan just looks.

97

At four-thirty, when he gets ready to go home to his kids, I lean over the edge of the loft bed and watch him get dressed. This time he shakes out his clothes before putting them on.

I'm at a day-care rally. A public hearing. I don't know what a public hearing is, but it seems to be a bunch of people who all want the same thing, who meet to tell why, while the adversaries never show up. We've just learned about the new fee scales proposed by Rockefeller for day-care centers. It's Tuesday night and last night I had a class and tomorrow night I have a class. Before I left the house Alex said, "You can't go out, you always go out." I know, but I really feel committed to work through this problem. What would I have done without day care? I'd be upstairs in the psych ward of St. Vincent's. President Nixon would like a resurgence of the nuclear family by making it impossible for women with children to support themselves or go to work. I'm in an uptown school auditorium, facing a table with rows of name tags of politicians, among them BELLA ABZUG, fiddling with my daughter's tape recorder, which her father gave her and which worked until this moment. I want to write an article and record all the speeches, but the thing won't work. "Cheap thing, cheap thing," I keep repeating over and over. Everyone agrees that these new rules oppress women, force them onto welfare, as they can't afford the new day-care fees, and when they are just about making a subsistence income they no longer qualify. Jeanette Washington says, "When they fool with our children, it's time to get mad, time to get bad."

I leave the hearing before the end. It's raining lightly, such tiny drops that they almost don't fall but hang in the air, blowing this way and that in the cold wind, getting stuck in my hair and filling it until it's an enormous halo of tumid curls. I'm in a hurry to listen to whether the tape recorder really did work. I do Rewind until somewhere in the middle, and I can't wait to hear whether a sound will really come from it or not. I hear the teary, almost inaudible woman's voice saying, ". . . and now, because of day care, I've finally been able to work and take care of my child, and now I won't qualify. Day care is all I have, and if they take it away . . ." Her voice breaks. "All I can say is . . . thank you, thank you for day care!"

I'm in my comparative-anatomy class. I've just thrown my dogfish shark away in the garbage, inside a plastic bag. Totally dissected, with my Barnes and Noble beginners' dissection kit, it looks like a flaked-tuna casserole. The man in my lab who sits behind me quietly rises and goes to get the professor. She follows him to his table and watches questioningly as silently he opens the pericardial cavity and spreads it where the mid-ventral incision is made, cranially from the abdomen, through the center of the pectoral girdle, and motions with his head for her to look inside. She does, and then laughs.
"What happened to it?"
"I don't know. It's missing. My lab partner must have taken it."
"What would he do with the heart? Voodoo?"
"Well, he's not here tonight, and the heart is gone."
"Use someone else's heart." He looks at me.
"I have none," I say, and go into the sink room, where a volunteer is opening a case of pickled cats. I'm ready for my cat. I choose a black-and-white one which looks exactly like my cat Dorothy at home, except this is wet, smells of formaldehyde, and is stiff as a board, arms and legs out, mouth open and tongue out, in a silent scream. I don't know whether I can start skinning him tonight without first going home and meditating on it for a week. "Oohh, that's disgusting," I say, looking at it through the plastic bag. From the looks I'm getting, I see that it's unusual for someone taking comparative anatomy to find these pickled cats disgusting. I wonder if this is a bad omen for my

99

grade—aside from the fact that I've just been informed that the professor wants to see our dogfish sharks and mine's already in the garbage.

Alan comes to pick me up after the class he teaches. We'd made a date to go to his apartment after class because he lives closer to Hunter, but now I don't feel like it. I'm feeling angry and very pressured. I've been out every night, I have an exam coming up, my house is a mess, I have to go to work tomorrow, and I want to write an article. I don't feel like going to make love with Alan, especially when things are so easy for him and so hard for me. The sight of him makes me angry, but it isn't his fault personally. I explain the whole day-care situation over coffee in a restaurant, trying to pretend there's nothing personal in my anger, which isn't true, but I dissimulate, directing my anger at circumstances. "I'm going home to do an article about it, and I have to study for an exam, and do the dishes . . . and I don't feel well."

"I understand," he says. "Write a good article."

Alan's holding my hand as we float through the warm, moist night, moving east on Sixty-third. Having no windshield wipers on my eyeglasses, I'm looking through myriad minuscule dots of moisture, creating pointillist paintings with my eyes.

"I really like this street," I say.

"Most of these are private houses," says Alan. "These people must be well connected."

"You're well enough connected," I answer, meaning that I think his apartment is quite nice enough, but he thinks I'm jokingly assessing his genitalia. He's holding the book I've given him to read, because I want to share it with him, gingerly, as if he'd like to give it back or drop it into the nearest litter basket. A few moments ago at the Fifty-ninth Street station, framed by Bloomingdale's windows, when I gave it to him, like handing him a revelation about myself, he accepted it with reservation. Wiping the moisture off his own eyeglasses with a large white hanky which he's whipped out of his coat pocket, a few puckers in the shape of Chinese silk tiedye spots where he'd blown his nose, but still bright white, from an excellent laundry, he stares at it earnestly. The frankly rounded, upside-down half-moon shape of his upper lip becomes more pronounced. He says, "Why this? Do you really want me to read this?"

"I really do, because I identify with it. I identify with George Jackson." He reads the copy off the back of the book, his large head with its black curls slightly tilted, a minute reflection from Bloomingdale's on his right temple.

" 'My credo is to seize the pig by the tusks and ride him till his neck breaks. If fortuitous outcome of circumstance allows him to prevail over me—again—then I want to have this carefully worked-up comment prepared. I want something to remain, to torment his ass, to haunt him, to make him know in no uncertain terms that he did incur this nigger's sore disfavor.' " He looks up at me with horror, head still tilted, his eyes moving over my open antique fur coat, with the wine-colored satin shirt glowing through the opening, my shiny black slacks, with their thin, thin red belt, and my slender, small-boned body on my platform pink-suede boots, my wild mass of hair around my tiny face, incredulous.

The candelabrum, made completely from elk's horns, is lit, the tiny precise flames reflecting on the shiny teak tabletop. Alan's children are at his mother's and mine are with their father, so I'm staying over, and he's making me a dinner. I'm sitting at the table, riffling through an old *New York Times* magazine section, sipping some red wine at the table left set for him by Louise. Alan appears, and puts on the table an ovenware dish full of steaming meat and noodles. It's a dinner called "casserole," and was previously prepared for him by Louise, who is a better cook than I am.

101

Has he ever considered marrying Louise? While I help him put the dishes into the dishwasher I say, "Want to see something?" I open my white sailcloth ecology shopping bag and pull out a plastic bag with a semi-dissected cat in it. "I'm taking it home to work on for the practical. I have to memorize every single artery, the whole venous system, the renal portal system, hepatic portal system, digestive system, urogenital system. . . ." I whip the cat out onto the Formica counter-top. There is an immediate smell of formaldehyde, not a passive odor but one which whips immediately into one's orifices, evoking tears. "Look at the blood vessels. Aren't they great?" They've been injected with latex, blue for the veins and red for the arteries. "Isn't it beautiful?"

"It's disgusting," he says, wrapping it up quickly. "Once the smell gets into the house, it's impossible to get rid of it." He smiles. Even he thinks it's disgusting, and he's a biologist. One thing I like about Alan is that though he's not crazy himself, he's very indulgent with me. He never tells me how to be. We talk some-times about how nice acceptance is and how long it takes to be able to have acceptance of the other person, the way they are, in a relationship.

We're sitting on one of the couches, our feet buried in the blue rug, a large round tumbler with a tiny bit of warm brandy fuming in the bottom, a dish of irregu-larly shaped brownies on the coffee table next to the brandy warmer.

"Have some brownies Louise made," says Alan.

"Do you tell Louise what to cook?" I ask.

"No. She wanted me to at first, but I just let her take over more and more. I really didn't care about those things."

I'm beginning to get a weird feeling. Strange, I identify with Louise, and I'm beginning to feel upset. I roll my golden brandy about the bottom of the glass. The taste doesn't flip me out, but its warmth is nice, and so is sitting on the couch, like a boat on a thick blue carpet, which is pleasantly dirty enough so that I don't feel that perhaps all his demands on Louise are too great. I slough off my boots like the old skin of a snake, and leave them, the pale pink suede floating in the rug, to go upstairs with Alan to his room, each carrying our brandy glasses like candles in a church procession.

I lie on the bed stiffly, feeling a sort of resentment which is disturbing, as I somehow think, like in a fairy tale, that this is the best relationship ever, so far. I want to continue to feel that way. He takes his box of Flair pens and chooses dark green. Beginning at the top edge of my dark pubic hair, he draws, in sketchy lines, two long green stems, switches to red, with which he makes two large flowers out of my breasts, then returns to green, finishing it off by connecting the stems more perfectly to the flowers, and making large, sketchy green leaves. I laugh. I'm impressed. It's pretty creative and shows he was thinking about it during the time we didn't see each other. My smile floats above his black curls as he buries his head into my chest and my nipple, which is a flower.

I'm looking forward to meeting his brother this morning, whom he hasn't seen in over a year, who's nine years younger and is having marriage problems with his beautiful Californian wife, who remained there, where he teaches economics. Alan is feeling hopeful about becoming closer with him, so I'm surprised that when Tim comes and we're having coffee, Alan talks about the weather. Their greeting was also very cool. I can't believe it, but no one mentions anything important that's happening in their lives. Perhaps it's because I'm there. I'd love to find out about Tim's wife and all about what's troubling them. At my suggestion, we go to see the Lucas Samaras show at the Whitney, which I loved, and, feeling spiteful, I want to see their reaction to that madness. As we leave, Alan says to

Tim and me, "I forgot to offer you some of Louise's apple brown betty."

Seated around the dark, spotless table at the Whitney cafeteria, I'm tracing the pattern on a doily that was under my three petit fours and my orange coffee with whipped cream, with a blue felt-tip pen that I have in my purse.

"Hey, that's not my Flair pen," says Alan.

"So I have a different kind of marker. Does that imply unfaithfulness?" Does that make him feel that I have a strange life aside from him, which he can't imagine?

They're talking. Tim says, "There are lots of things wrong with this country. For instance, certainly something could be done with the postal system."

"What?" I say, butting in.

"Yes, the system is terrible," Alan agrees.

"Certainly, with better management of funds and taxes, it could be remedied."

"I can't believe it . . . of all the things wrong with this country you complain about the postal service? Are you mad? What about socialized medicine? Don't you think everyone has the right to good medical care? What about day care?" I've been turning purple, and neither of them answers me. We discuss psychotherapy, which I know Alan doesn't believe in, and which I always bring up when I feel like arguing.

Alan says, "I don't believe in therapy. It does more harm than good. I'm perfectly satisfied with myself. People should do more about keeping busy than spend all that energy on introspection and self-obsession."

"The fact that you're so satisfied with yourself seems a bit suspect to me," I say. "What about another area, such as relationships? Don't you sometimes feel that there's some secret to them that you can't quite put your finger on, that's missing in your own relationships?"

"Yes," he says softly. I appreciate his honesty. Tim gets up from the table without a word. I think he's annoyed with me. We find him later, buying a Lucas

Samaras poster. Contrary to being bugged, he liked the show. It's freezing out. We take a cab to Sixty-third Street and I remain in the taxi to go downtown. We all feel very warm toward each other. I really feel affection for Alan and kiss him goodbye. They each hold out two dollars for the fare, and I take the money from both of them; it'll cost at least three dollars to get downtown.

We're in a luncheonette, waiting for the ten o'clock show of *Cries and Whispers*. The sight of Alan is irritating to me and I don't know why. It makes me feel insane. We're sitting there having coffee, while the black waiter smiles at me above Alan's black hair. His shirt irritates me, his slacks, his socks. I feel terrible. Prejudiced. I wouldn't appreciate his own gaze to rove over my clothing with the same kind of prejudice. He's reading the newspaper we bought in order to find out what's playing, and I'm drinking coffee, watching him with my critical gaze. Yet I don't want him to look up because I don't want to relate to him. We're like an old married couple who're bored with each other. He's reading about a resurgence of the gangs in the south Bronx. He tells me that Louise has lived in the south Bronx since she came here from Jamaica, but now she's moving because things are so bad, like with the Grim Reapers and stuff. He says, "There's a direct correlation between the decrease in drug addiction and the rise of these street gangs, like the ones we had in the fifties." I wonder if he's advocating drugs. "It's terrible," he says. "What can be done?"

"Nothing, until we change society," I say. I agree that it's terrible, but I think we both see it as terrible from different directions. "I understand those kids, why they have gangs. I understand their violence stemming from impotence. They know they have no home for any identity or fulfillment or escape from their own poverty-stricken lives. Instead of living like their parents, they choose another way out: they create their own society, where they're all accepted. I used to belong to a gang when I was sixteen," I reveal, in a complicitory tone.

"You did?" he says as he beckons the waiter for more coffee.

"Yes. We had a motorcycle gang in Brooklyn. We all had jackets. Of course it wasn't the girls' gang, we each had a boyfriend. I had a blood pact with mine. We cut our arms and put them together. I was terrified to leave him."

"Really?"

"No, I'm just putting you on. I really belonged to a fake sorority."

"Can I borrow five dollars?" he asks. "I haven't got enough for the movies."

"I'll be glad to pay for myself tonight."

"Don't be silly; lend me the money and I'll pay for you. I have more money than you."

I think it over. Is it socialism? I leave an enormous tip for the waiter as Alan gets my coat, and he helps me put it on even though I'm trying to grab it away from him. I rush up to the cashier and pay the forty-cent bill.

Later, when we get up to leave the movie theater, still in a daze from *Cries and Whispers*, I pick up Alan's coat from the seat, hold it open, soft lamb lining facing him, and ease it over his shoulders, awkwardly, as he's tall. He doesn't know whether to laugh, or what to do about this brand of sarcasm. I feel sorry for him, but I'm powerless to stop. He looks at me searchingly. "That was sure a depressing picture!" I don't want him to think it's the picture that's causing me to be depressed. It isn't.

We're sitting on my studio couch. His eyes keep rolling up toward my sleeping loft and his tongue is hanging out to the floor, but I don't feel like going to bed with him. I'm still feeling angry. At what I'm not sure. So I heat some chili that we had for dinner and put it into two of the new bowls I bought. It sits there in the middle of the bowl, thick, unmoving. I break saltines over it but it remains impervious. I have to press the saltines in.

"What do you use for chili, a fork or a spoon?" I ask.

"A spoon, silly."

For my chili, it really doesn't matter.

"This is good chili."

"Louise made it," I say. Again, he looks at me with puzzlement.

"What's bothering you?" he says.

I think for a while, but I really don't know. "I don't know."

"I thought we accepted each other."

"I thought so too, but maybe as our relationship advances, we can't afford to without ignoring issues which are a large part of our make-up. I can't always be expected to be happy and ready for you when we have a date, to have a good time and then go home and be horny all the time and ready to make love at the right time like a computer."

"Well, at the present time that's the best we can do because of our kids and our work and all. That's how our lives are defined."

All the time he's eating chili. It annoys me because he makes me wait long periods of time for answers or replies, while he chews.

"This is good chili," he says.

"But it's not strong enough."

"I know, it needs more chili powder."

"Well, tell Louise, she made it."

Silence except for the sound of eating.

"I like your red sheet."

"It's not red, it's hot pink."

His bowl, empty now except for the track marks of spoon scrapings, from his last fracas with the stubborn stuff, remains. He burps. He's getting nervous that he won't get laid. He's thinking that I'm still angry and

107

he keeps looking up at the loft bed, wondering how he can calm me down within a reasonable amount of time. I notice that, chili gone, his consciousness of the empty dish disappears, he's so used to being served. I want so badly to tell him to get up and put it in the sink, but I almost can't bear being so nasty. I sit there a moment in conflict because keeping silent is bothering me also. I really feel unhappy. I can't leave it.

"Does Louise serve you your dinners?" I ask.

"Yes, sure."

"She actually puts the dishes in front of you and you just sit there?"

"Yes. Why?"

"How many hours a week less does she work than you? Or does she work more hours? I've been seeing Louise, and together we're organizing a housekeepers' union."

His crescent lip becomes rounder.

"But I've never seen Louise; maybe she doesn't really exist. Perhaps she's just a spirit." I really haven't seen Louise, as she's never there on weekends or at night, unless Alan is out. I've only eaten her cooking. He smiles . . . he thinks it's going to be okay, and soon . . . the loft bed.

"Speaking of spirits," he says, "Louise is very cute. She's really very superstitious. When we moved into my apartment, and we had all the stuff all around us, and the moving men had driven off, she said, 'And now, Dr. Linart, let's say a prayer for the house.' " He's smiling deeply; his dimple inverts.

"She calls you 'Doctor'?" I ask, incredulous.

"She wants to," he says.

I'm wondering whether he's simply become a political adversary by being a man. In a panic, I run through all my girl friends, trying to imagine which ones I might have a sexual relationship with in case I can't be civil to men anymore.

"I'd really like to go up that sleeping loft with you," he says.

108

I think, how come I never cared so much about all these differences before? "I can't sleep with you tonight," I say. "It's like Angela Davis making it with Rockefeller." I'm feeling thoroughly miserable, have a case of hives, and feel my asthma coming on.

He looks at me, puzzled and hurt. "Do our political differences have to affect our relationship?"

THE RAPE

Mrs. Green heard a voice from the outside, so, with enormous effort, and trembling, she extracted her head from inside her cunt, where she spent most of her time lately because she had a better vantage point there for viewing her multi body processes. The nurse came in just in time to see the bald head of Mrs. Green, a little moist, peering over the top of the dresser drawer, in the old bureau she was so fond of that she refused to sleep anywhere else, and wobbling slightly, like that of a newborn baby.

"Good morning," she said.

"Oh, is it morning?" asked Mrs. Green.

The nurse didn't understand what Mrs. Green said, probably because Mrs. Green had no teeth and very little gums, and portions of her larynx had been removed in an operation some years prior to her admittance to the Home for the Aged. Mrs. Green couldn't keep track of the days anyway. The nurse pulled up the green shades and said how lucky Mrs. Green was to have such a nice back room with some shrubbery to look at if she could see, but it really didn't matter because Mrs. Green never left her drawer except when she was carried to the dining room. Perhaps a "good morning" from these crude nurses who said good morning even when it wasn't a good morning—when it was raining, snowing, or when one's functions weren't working—was better than nothing, even if it was false. And it was, since the nurse wasn't happy to see Mrs. Green.

No one wanted to see Mrs. Green anymore. Her inability to care for herself had been the cause of the separation of all her children. In their zeal not to have Mrs. Green with them, they had endless disagreements and none of them spoke to each other anymore. Her daughter in East Meadow put Mrs. Green out with the garbage one morning, but luckily she was seen through the new green plastic garbage bags and, being found still alive, was brought to the nursing home, where she spent two years in the lobby waiting for a room, hunched into a corner of a wheelchair. And no one said good morning until it was established who was to pay the bill for her room and board. But Mrs. Green was no bother to anybody; she just sat there curled into a ball, her head up her womb, as usual, no one bothering to feed her, clean her, and take her to the toilet. She would have screamed if her larynx had been in better condition, or even in existence.

Now Mrs. Green was in a beautiful room which she couldn't see, and she had her own furniture, which she wouldn't part with until death, and she had plans of possibly remaining with it after death, all depending upon what that was like.

She suspected that death was nothing, as she suspected that life was nothing. She didn't even want herself anymore, yet she watched herself every minute of the day and night with great zeal to see that she was still alive, no matter in what condition. She never slept, because she knew that if she wasn't watching her body she'd probably die, an event which she wished for and feared. She didn't know whether she desired death or just wished that dying were over. Or that life were over. She was weary of it; it was so damn dis-

111

appointing for a romantic person like Mrs. Green. On the other hand, Mrs. Green didn't want to die. She never so much wanted to live as now. Though in her youth she had often wished to die, now she never let up her vigil because she loved life more than ever. She finally had peace; she'd reached herself, what she really was, an organism, and it was joyful after all those years full of bullshit and heartaches to find herself in delicious organism, a magnificent creature of functions.

The day was full of her functions from morning to night and through the night, never boring, functions so vital and meaningful—only to herself, of course. The nurse—was it the same nurse?—could never understand why Mrs. Green couldn't find the energy to place a streak of red lipstick across her slack, wrinkled, white lips, hanging in summer, tight and cracked in winter. She insisted, "You'll feel so much better. Do look in the mirror, straighten your skirt, Mrs. Green, that's a good girl." What did Mrs. Green care if her skirt was straight, crooked, backward, or inside out? And to look into a mirror . . . what for? The sight of Mrs. Green to Mrs. Green was as meaningless as it was meaningful. Was that herself in the mirror? It was as much not herself as it was. Improbable that her image was really Valerie Green. That was not Valerie Green just as much as the former states, the ephemeral states, the ones that had gone, were not Valerie Green. Just as much as they were Valerie Green, they were not. When forced by that stupid, coarse, insensitive nurse, or nurses, the ones who changed her diapers, to look into the mirror, Mrs. Green saw only a shadow, with her ten-percent vision, of her bald head, and other formless features. Once she'd had a chin, but no longer. It had either been absorbed by her neck or was being covered by her lower lip, now so slack that it actually hung down that far, but Mrs. Green didn't even have the desire to lift up her lip to possibly discover her lost chin, even if she had the use of her hands, which she

112

couldn't move anymore, but which, the fingers spread out stiffly, like two fans, she could still amuse herself with, when she had nothing to do, even if only from habit, since she didn't really want to anymore.

"Mrs. Green, playing with yourself again, you should be ashamed!" Mrs. Green couldn't figure out why she should be ashamed of that when she wasn't ashamed of anything anymore.

Her farts could be heard long into the night. In fact, farting was one of Mrs. Green's most pungent pleasures, which she played to the utmost of luxuriousness and variation; by the simple tightening and loosening of her sphincter muscle she could achieve exactly, or pretty nearly, the kind of fart that she liked, her favorite being a great, large, smooth puff lasting a full three minutes or so, the culmination slightly undefined. This was done by total relaxation of the sphincter, Mrs. Green's sphincter having the added embellishments of many hemorrhoids, creating different variations of sound, like hanging wind chimes. Mrs. Green could save gas for this favorite fart for days if she wanted a splendid one, for a lot of gas for this one was a must, and usually the aroma was a rich, deep, heady one. Other favorites were what she called surprise farts, the unexpected ones, some silent, that she wouldn't even know they were there until she sniffed her own heady aroma, which she could tell from all others, and which varied from fart to fart but had a certain characteristic that made itself recognizable to her as purely hers, and perhaps to others too. Mrs. Green could barely see, was totally deaf, the skin of her stiff, fanlike hands was like thin moroccan leather, but her sense of smell was still intact. At certain times she enjoyed the smell of the fresh air from the small courtyard, concrete, with a few hedges, weeds between the concrete cracks, and bits of broken glass around the edges, but she still preferred the more decadent smells of her own body at this stage in her life. It was to further that enjoy-

113

ment that she changed her beloved oilcloth linings of the drawer where she slept—the white oilcloth with its familiar oilcloth smell and its repeated pattern of three red Bing cherries, with a bit of sparkling reflection in the form of a yellow rectangle on the round part of each cherry, the cheeks separated by a cleft from which sprung a stem, so that every group looked like three backsides with three tails held together by a pink bow. Now she had soft cotton batting. With the oilcloth, which was so totally nonabsorbent, the effluvia dispersed very quickly in a short burst, and the moisture in the drawer was not good for Mrs. Green's asthma, but if she wished to with the cotton she could fart directly into it, and the fart would be absorbed and preserved in little pockets of fragrance, which could be referred to at any time. Related to farting was another of Mrs. Green's pleasures, defecating. In fact, sometimes she got the two confused until she was confronted with the end result.

Mrs. Green had two very thin, pure-white legs with large blue veins, but their length was indeterminate because she used them so rarely that they were never stretched out. She used to try to get out of the drawer to go to the bathroom; but could never make it in time, since she had to push the drawer out far enough for her body, which was centrally very obese, to emerge, a fact which was discovered by the person or persons who cleaned Mrs. Green and her drawer, who brought her the mouthwash for her rancid tongue and gums, who opened and closed her windows—the one with the gate on it and the one without—and, after scolding was to no avail, diapers were employed, but much of the time Mrs. Green spent fooling around inside the diaper, and when it became too difficult, she actually took out the pins very carefully with her stiff fingers and stuck them neatly into the cotton lining of her drawer, as she'd always done all her life with pins and needles, and threw the diaper aside. This exasperated her present nurse, who put in an application to be removed from Mrs. Green's charge, but nothing was being done about it soon enough. The nurses were going to bring it up at a meeting of the staff, only the directors were refurnishing the meeting room and spent every meeting attempting to decide whether they should have a wooden table or Formica and chrome.

She didn't even know why she bothered to play with herself; she really didn't even enjoy it anymore. It was either bordom or habit, and sometimes she had to work at it for as much as three hours or more without any result, and had to conjure up timeworn fantasies that no longer interested her. She much preferred defecating to masturbating, any day. Even though it was sometimes painful with her hemorrhoids, Mrs. Green felt that it was worth it. She enjoyed measuring the pain against the pleasure even while it was happening. She probably even enjoyed the pain. She knew from the births of her children exactly how to breathe and push—the main thing for which she was thankful that she'd had children.

The nurse took Mrs. Green to the dining room for meals in a wheelchair now, because when she used to walk in, after being notified of a mealtime, sometimes it took her so long to emerge from her drawer and actually get to the dining room, which smelled of disinfectant and tomato-vegetable soup—and sometimes she actually lost her way—mealtime was over and she lay across the linoleum-covered tables and wept because at her age, with a spastic colon and ulcer, even though she could hardly eat anything without getting a stomachache, missing a meal was one of the only things that frightened Mrs. Green. She didn't care whether she ate shepherd's pie or oatmeal, though her favorite was mashed potatoes mixed with peas, a mixture she effected with her fingers; then she enjoyed squeezing the pulp from the pea skin by pressing her stiff forefinger on the pea and the inside squooshed out, very beautifully,

115

she thought. Her neighbors on the benches didn't agree. When she did eat, Mrs. Green ate with her hands, since she couldn't manipulate utensils. She scooped with one or more fingers, no matter what the consistency of the food. Some always fell on her nightgown, the front of which at the end of the day was a stiff crust from chin to cunt, some food fell down, as she often missed her mouth entirely, the contour of it being so undefined and her aim was poor, and some dribbled out, as she had no teeth and only part of a throat. Just the process of eating comforted her even if not too much got in, then she would be taken to her room to digest. A petition was being passed around the dining hall requesting that Mrs. Green be given her food in her room and be permanently excused from the dining room on the grounds that being in her company during meals demolished the appetites of all. Mrs. Green couldn't balance on her backside in a sitting position, for which she was requisitioned a rubber tire to sit in. She ended up leaning precariously against either one of the neighbors. The maintenance man who cleaned up the dining room complained that, after he picked up Mrs. Green by pushing her onto the large dustpan with the dustbrush and into her wheelchair, the area where she'd eaten was too filthy. Also, the dustbrushes were ruined with grease and moisture.

This particular evening after she had been wheeled into her room and placed in her drawer, Mrs. Green, the lamp still on, was comfortably engrossed in observing her digestive processes. Curled up cozily, her head in her cunt, she could watch the procedure of digestion all the way from her esophagus to the stomach, the large intestine and the small; she could observe the gall bladder and the pancreas, see the liver storing the glucose as glycogen, and observe the proper passage of wastes through to her kidneys, bladder, ureter, and lower bowel. She kept a keen eye on her appendix, which she still retained through thick and thin, even

116

though one kidney and most of her large intestine had been removed. It was particularly moist and musty for Mrs. Green's asthma, but she had inserted her head inside her body not only to guard against an error of digestion on the part of one of her organs, but also—mainly—because she couldn't resist doing it; in fact, could barely make out her organs anymore. She often thought that if she was not so arthritic she would be able to push beyond, and twist double and push her whole body right into her uterus, where she imagined total peace.

Outside her window, in the dusk, in which her lamp-lit room showed like an oasis of warmth and light, a man was jerking off violently, leaning just his shoulder against the wooden frame of the window without the gate. He'd just happened to be there behind the nursing home and had seen Mrs. Green being helped into the top drawer of her carved bureau in two tones of warm brown, and it occurred to him to masturbate, he knew not why. It appeared to him to have nothing at all to do with Mrs. Green, who was not being very enticing, and not masturbating herself at the time, it was not the sight of her stiff hands separating her soft loose lips with the sparse, curly beards.

It was just a sudden thought of the evening, and at the time he thought he could just as well ignore the idea and walk away; it was not actually a compulsion, but since he could just as well ignore the thought of masturbating, why not not ignore it? It was all the same, so, with fingers trembling with desire of himself, he unzipped his fly and took out his cock, which in itself was not too enthusiastic and accordian-pleated at the touch of his chilly hands. For a moment the man entertained again the thought of putting away his peter and leaving; he tested for a moment in his mind whether it would be easy for him to do that or whether he was compelled to continue this act. Since his fly was already open, and because he felt that he could close his fly and walk away, he decided to stay and finish. He made his fat index finger and thumb into the shape of a wedding ring, which he slipped on his member. It barely fit around because his fingers were extremely short and stubby, and so was his cock. The accordian pleats began to expand and warm his hand as he accelerated those movements of his hand, which nevertheless did not seem to move from its position right under the mushroom head of his prick. His buttocks tightened and moved forward, his face was red and double-chinned with strain, he moved that ring of two fingers, the sign that all is well, faster, faster . . . then for a moment he stopped, breathing hard, started again, stopped, then started faster than ever, and a stupid, glassy, totally idiotic expression, vapid, glassy-eyed, came over his face and remained for a moment as his hand shuddered. His cock spat three separate wads all over Mrs. Green's window, each one smaller than the last, and a bit more liquid. The man looked at those three spots in surprise, then opened the ring of his fingers, slowly. Totally drained, he seemed to disappear. The top spot, which remained on the window like a firm jelly, began to dry, while some liquid dripped down from it slowly, reaching the second spot, which was more liquid, and both quickly ran down, down the rest of the length of the windowpane in a weird, irregular line which glowed greenly in the dusk.

When Mrs. Green's nurse came to pull the shade, she said she guessed that some of the birds in the area had diarrhea. She was in a good mood because she thought that possibly she wouldn't be seeing Mrs. Green much longer because their meeting table was arriving the next day, if all went well, an Italian Provincial, antique white, with a wood-grain Formica top. The next morning Mrs. Green's nurse noticed that what she thought was bird shit had already hardened, but she didn't care. It wasn't her job to clean the windows. The meeting hadn't gone well, even though the table was

118

a success. They couldn't resolve the matter of all those who had put in for transfers. Even if they were to hire special people who would agree beforehand to the duties of caring for Mrs. Green, it would take time. This morning, out of spite, she didn't bring Mrs. Green her mouthwash, didn't wash her down, just changed her diaper, with an accompaniment of many expressions of disgust, some verbal, others merely primitive sounds. The death of Mrs. Green would be a welcome event to her. That day, due to her nurses' rebellion, Mrs. Green remained in comparative squalor. Though she did receive her meals, she wasn't washed, her diaper was changed only once, and, in total abandonment, Mrs. Green dispensed with the diaper altogether. She sensed the nurses' resentment of her and felt very uneasy.

It was not a dark night when the man returned to the small courtyard off Mrs. Green's room. Though it was late and all the lights were out in the old-ladies' nursing home, Mrs. Green's shade hadn't been lowered and he could catch a glimpse of her form, wormlike, churning slowly in her drawer. He couldn't say why he'd returned. It wasn't until he began opening his fly and this time pulling down his pants that he realized he was going to masturbate again. He began to anticipate it, but he was damp and cold and, jerk as he might, after the first excitement at the thought of the act, he could get no more pleasure from it. He struggled and struggled to revive the excitement. He even stopped, removing his hand from his penis for a moment, trying to recapture in his mind his desire; then, when he thought he had it, he began slowly, but by the time he was moving his hand quickly he'd lost the thread of pleasure again, and stopped, frustrated. All of a sudden he thought of ravishing Mrs. Green, and he breathed involuntarily, two jerky, convulsive breaths, neither of which satisfied his need for oxygen. It wasn't Mrs. Green in particular that he desired, it was her resistance which he pictured, which excited him so much that his whole body felt suddenly hot and swollen, his cock so much so that it seemed as if his body could no longer support such a weight against the force of gravity. He opened the window cautiously, for he had no idea of the degree of Mrs. Green's decrepitude. He climbed in carefully and easily, except for the trouble caused by forgetting to pull his pants all the way up, and when he tried to lift his leg to reach the sill he was almost pulled out from underneath by his own pants. After grazing his balls a bit on the stone outside sill, he attained entry without further mishap. Mrs. Green was not sleeping; nevertheless she was surprised to see him standing over her drawer, looking at her, and possessing an enormous erection. In fact, this enormous erection was just about resting on the top of the drawer in which resided Mrs. Green, was practically hanging over her. Mrs. Green's faulty vision distorted this member, made the edges diaphanous, causing it to appear even larger and less hard. Like a cloud. Maybe this was heaven, she thought. In spite of distortion, she recognized this object, one of the interests of her youth, and, lying in her humid drawer, she felt all her orifices grow tumid. The man himself she could hardly see, nor did things like that interest her anymore, but he wasn't bad-looking, at any rate, for he had beautiful black wavy hair with a lovely sheen or too much grease, and beautiful blue eyes, so what did it matter if his head was a bit flat and that he had almost no forehead at all, it was almost impossible to differentiate his eyebrows from his hairline. For a moment he couldn't decide whether to hop into the drawer or take Mrs. Green out. He decided to take the drawer out of its socket in the dresser and place it on the floor, all the time in a flurry of panic, praying for Mrs. Green to continue in shock, which was what he thought ailed her and was the cause of her silence, not knowing, of course, that she had no larynx. He stood over the

120

drawer which enclosed Mrs. Green and pressed the upper part of his body over hers, holding her shoulders back with all the force of his upper torso, which was huge. Then the rest of him hopped on Mrs. Green, and his legs were so short in comparison with the rest of his body that he practically fit into the drawer himself. Mrs. Green, responding to the weight of this sheer physical insistence, was flooded by an exotic passion deeper than she had ever known, and was never so anxious to yield. Coupled with this fantastic feeling was his weight pressing on her swollen belly, squeezing all the annoying gas out of her in one enormous, exotic fart. He entered her gaping cunt, gaping in ordinary circumstances, so much more so now, with ease, and quickly slid in. Since he'd been expecting some resistance from one quarter or another, he lay there on Mrs. Green for a moment, disoriented, while Mrs. Green, feeling someone desire her so much, was experiencing the greatest joy, and she began to moan and gyrate her arthritic hips. The man, so absolutely disgusted by her yielding consilience, was at first tempted to vomit, then to withdraw and leave, but he was so angry at having troubled, and been frustrated, for nothing, that he thought of beating a bit of resistance into Mrs. Green, thereby making it exciting once more, so he smacked her face to and fro, while still in her. Blood from her lips ran down and mingled with tomato-soup stains on the nightshirt, now wrapped around her neck, but her eyes just rolled up into their sockets with ecstasy, so he beat her more and more. It wasn't clear to him when she might have died; he was so angry with her that he continued to beat her really with vengeance, the more passive she was; then he stood over her and jerked himself off, all three spurts falling on Mrs. Green's wide, beatific smile. He covered her annoyingly smiling head with the pillow and smothered her dead body for a while, then took out his penknife

121

and made a few cuts. He remembered to pull up his pants and left by the window, closing it before he disappeared.

THE LOVER

I told him I had to go but he poured the charcoal lighter fluid all over the charcoal anyway, in large squirts, from a distance, by pressing the can. It was like thick urine, or sperm, a magnificent come, in four or five spurts, and now it lay there on top of the charcoal, thick and milky, bluish or grayish, the issue of the great suburban fuck, a last reproof for my wanting to go somewhere. Herbert picked up the barbecue sauce from the sticky tray table his mother bought us, with a picture of the same Vermont scene with orange, yellow, red, and brown Halloween trees reflected also in an obsoletely clean and glistening stream, the same scene on every street for the past thirty years in the Washington Square Outdoor Art Show. I thought I'd barf if I had to see it one more time. Portions of it were already covered with old, sticky stains of previous sauces of previous barbecues, but a different kind of sauce.

But it was still good of his mother to bring it, wasn't it? That's why we'd have it forever. She still brought her son his favorite goodies every Saturday. Well, if she wanted him back she could have him. He married me because I'm so different from her, now he complains because I don't look like her, but he doesn't realize it. His mother is very fat, has enormous breasts, small blue eyes, and hair so straight that it's responsive only to gravity. The only thing she and I both have is a big mouth. She sluffs heavily about in tights, tight skirts, blouses that gape between each button, in flat. slippers. I'd always been triumphant, I never thought of her as a threat, until now, I realize that it was I who posed no threat, I who should have been jealous all along. I had thought that my youth and sexy qualities could come between a relationship of nineteen years' duration. At first he liked me because I'm thin, small, with dark eyes and very curly masses of hair. Then, after we married, he says, "Why can't you have bigger breasts, why don't you have a bigger ass, why don't you eat more, why is your hair so messy? Let it grow." In other words, "Why don't you look more like mom?" But he says, instead, "If you looked more like Marilyn Monroe you'd turn me on more." I guess that's more acceptable.

Well, I could picture them together. She's practically in the room with us all the time anyway. He'd lie there on the bed, only his eyes moving, and the one hand with which he very deftly goes into his fly and pursues his penis, pulls it out, and waits, passive. His penis, emerged from the slit of his fly, lies limply, curled over, sticking out like a piece of garlic from a slit in a veal roast, and gently moves. His mother gets undressed, one fat arm shielding her giant nipples shyly as she pulls the tight but enormous black skirt down over her worn scuffs. Herb lies there, his penis erect now, the only vertical thing on his horizontal body, pointing slightly at his face, which is slack and tense at the same time, appearing twice as wide as usual with the strain of his neck muscles, his tiny light eyes still moving lecherously, but not sensuously. Even in sex his eyes retain their infantile quality. One thick hand curls around his rod as if it's cupping a stein of beer, and he begins to move it up and down. Ida pulls out her

124

stringy bun and lets her hair hang down, along with
the rest of her. She floats heavily over to the bed and
lies down. They are both lying there side by side,
breathing hard, passive. He grabs her breast and begins
jerking off more quickly, the top of his cock shining
with strain.

"Are you my slave?" he asks.

"Oh," she cries, with no poise at all, "I forgot, the
schav is burning, and the prokis, and the sweet
potatoes." She disembogues herself from the bed in
a clumsy flurry, gets into her scuffs, and goes into the
kitchen. Herb is lying there, still, cock purple and
shiny, his other thumb in his mouth, just waiting. She
is standing in the doorway now, completely naked,
triumphant, holding a huge bowl of sweet-and-sour
cabbage, and wiggles her ass a little.

"Wiggle your ass," he says. She moves shyly but
proudly. He's jerking off harder now, his whole body
curved at the same angle as his cock, only two fingers
moving swiftly beyond the speed of sound, as the other
fingers flare out like a fan, cooling his pubic hair. He
remains tense but his hand stops. She gives another
wiggle in the doorway, the smoke drifting off the top
of the prokis. He moves his hand once again, stops,
then harder. He looks as if he's ready to explode.
She says, "Hurry, while it's hot," and he does explode,
fluid spurting in four or five squirts onto the black
hair on his stomach, as his body becomes flaccid.

For that matter, my mother is practically in the room
when we make love too. Herb is lying on the bed,
hairy and naked, in the same position. My mother is
sitting in the butterfly chair, complaining that she can't
get out of it, as Herb is saying, "Cup your breasts."
I pull my T-shirt over my head, and my mother says,
"Don't you ever comb your hair?" Herb says, "Wiggle
it, baby, dance." I do my best. I can see that I excite
him, he's like a burnt roast beef, sizzling and spatter-
ing. My mother is shaking her jowls, saying, "You'll

never do it; with your hair like that, and that kind of
clothes, you'll be here all day." And I, knowing that
it's okay to feel pleasure, just not to show it, am
dancing happily, glad not to be put in a position of
responding to anyone. He comes.

"See? I told you, mother, he likes my hair this way."

"Well, he'd come quicker if you combed it."

"Goddamnit, I don't like this barbecue sauce, it's the
wrong kind. You know what kind I like. How could
you get the wrong kind?"

"It was the only one they had at the A&P when I
went shopping."

"Well, it's better to get nothing than the wrong kind."

"But I don't like to go to fifty different stores to get
all the different right things. What does it matter? It
really depresses me, there's always something else to
get. My mind is full all day of stuff to get, making me
tense, and it's all trivia."

"But it's important. How can you say it's trivia?
Besides, what else do you have to do all day?"

"The store where they have the sauce you like is
too expensive."

"I told you, money is no object."

"No, not where it comes to food."

"What do you have against good food? You don't
want me to have any pleasure, you're such a Spartan.
Go get another bottle of sauce. The right kind this
time."

"Why can't we use the one we have? All this fuss
about barbecue sauce is so petty."

"We don't have it anymore!" he shouts, as he throws
the bottle off the terrace, against the wall of the apartment building next to us. The glass shatters, leaving a
large red splash which gently drips down. (It's the
watery kind.)

"Saucy Susan, Saucy Susan," he screams in his ugly
way, his thick lips, thicker in tantrum, back over his
teeth, his front teeth with the space and the one cracked

126

where a kid once pushed his face into a water fountain. I used to feel sorry for him when he told me about it, but now I felt triumphant.

I went to the store. I don't know why I was afraid of him. He was loud, but he never hit me. He was enormous, with broad shoulders, and very hairy, with black hair like icing all over his body, including his shoulders, which made them appear even larger. After he shaved there was a neat line of hair around his neck, tendrils curling neatly around the stem of his thick neck like a hair T-shirt, or like the pubic hair around the stem of his cock. His legs were thin, the only part of him that he felt was weak, making too much walking prohibitive.

I hurried, sullenly, over to the Opera Deli, which was open seven days a week, twenty-four hours a day, and where they charged (on Sunday) five dollars for a bottle of Saucy Susan. Herb pushed the hair off his forehead with an exultant and affected gesture when I returned with the sauce. He struck a match.

"Listen, I told you not to light it. I have to go. I have an appointment with Narcissa."

"Why do you have to see Narcissa on Sunday? She's so fat."

"What does Sunday have to do with it? You're home every day. You work at home. It's not as if I never see you." I ran down the stairs feeling that I owed him nothing because I'd bought the Saucy Susan.

Before I entered the familiar subway station I automatically looked behind me. If for some reason he'd followed me out or went to get something, it wouldn't do to have him see me enter the subway. One thing about Herb was that he wasn't suspicious. I only had to travel two stations on the D train downtown to be in a totally different environment, the funky Lower East Side, and a romantic assignation. As I absently

127

pushed my way into the train I thought I saw Herb enter the same car, through the other door. I thought I imagined it, but to make sure I went into the next car. And a moment later, peering at me from in between many people, his hairy arm depending from behind someone's purple shirt, half his face towering above a woman's upsweep, fragmented, but there, was Herb. He didn't move. For some reason, he was content to stand there and let me know that he saw me. He made no move to come over, just shrugged the hair out of his eyes in that affected way he had. I was filled with anger, fear, and spite. I knew I'd go through with my appointment anyway. I had some integrity. I got out of the train at Allen Street and walked east on Houston toward Avenue C, the heavy September sun shining twice as bright as ever reflected through the heavy, moist air until the sunlight itself became heavy, part of the thick atmosphere. I was broiling in my T-shirt.

"Ragamuffin," a bum calls. Who is he to talk? I think. But it's true. I have no standard of appearance other than sensuousness, no matter how sloppy.

I'm ready to burst from the tension, because Herb is still following me, remaining about a block behind, certainly aware that I know he's following, yet refusing to confront me. I'm more than ever compelled to fulfill my assignation. My obstinacy fills me so much that I'm totally swollen, as if I would soon burst, and the sun beating down on me might cause it, then I'll just lie there like another piece of garbage, Lower East Side maggots inhabiting my rent-free body. Finally he screams, "Come on home. Don't do this to me. You'll be sorry." He screams behind me, but he comes no closer. I turn onto a half-demolished block. The back-yards of all the houses are exposed because half the street's already been torn away. It looks like a cross section made with an uneasy scalpel, exposing all the innards. The moist mushroom atmosphere is pene-trating, the dried plaster dust and brick pushing their

128

ancient molecules into the air, turning it to lead poison, mushroom, and urine soup. I go up stairs, so familiar that I don't even know the address anymore, passing exposed sweating pipes somehow as obscene as a person exposing himself in the semigloom. Cooking smells mingle with the plaster smells in one giant, turbulent odor soup, thick and immovable. The walls are the color of split-pea soup, steamed-cabbage green, corned-beef pink, all steaming hot. One flight up, there is Sam, short, balding, trim, and sexy, waiting for me, shirtless, the upper portion of him hairless, his whole body glistening like the head of Herb's cock. As yet he has no conception of the surprise I've brought. He smiled a joyless smile; it's a serious love he feels for me. A joyless love, lacking humor. It's dark and deep, heavy, heavy. I felt it ponderous upon me immediately. He kissed me and I became more and more weighted, but I didn't feel anything else except aesthetic appreciation of his green eyes in his dark-skinned face. We stood in the kitchen, the one merit of which was that it was large. It was also the most renovated room, having a built-in counter. There was a bowl of cherries on the counter, and Greek salad with feta and black olives. I knew his mother made the cheese. He sensed something.

"What's wrong? Don't you love me?"

All of a sudden we heard a voice shouting through the window of the front room, "Come down, Lynda, you come on down right now!"

Sam looks at me. His eyes have popped from his skull, have risen on his bald forehead, glistening, the black of his pupils dilating and obliterating all the green. But no, it's only momentary shock. In reality he's going to enjoy this. He's half the size of Herb both longitudinally and latitudinally, with no protective coating of hair.

"Herb?" Sam asks.

"Come home with me. Come down here. Come on home! Send her down, you bastard," Herb yells.

I motion for Sam to ignore him, but Sam the big shot yells, "She's not coming home."

"Lynda, please," Herb yells, "please. I'm leaving this minute. If I go home without you you'll be sorry."

I want to ask exactly how I'll be sorry. I'd like to know what's in store, but I haven't the courage to find out. Nevertheless, I'm powerless to go down, nor do I want to. I just sit and gobble cherries. From the front room I hear, "Ooohh, oooohhhhhh, ooooooohhhhhhhhhh, oooooooooooohhhhhhhhhhhhhhhh." Silence. It's Narcissa, in Joe's room, having an orgasm. I thought she told me she couldn't come. Sounds to me like she's finally made it.

"I'm going now. You'll be sorry for this irreparable rift!" For a second I feel torn, ripped, in more ways than one, yet I won't leave. Sam holds me. I feel nothing. I eat more cherries. He takes one.

"I bought them for you," he says. I'm glad, because I've eaten them all.

"I hope he doesn't let you in when you get home. Have some salad and cheese."

"No, thanks."

He kisses me more. I decide to make love with him to see whether I'll feel more this time. The bed is moved away from the wall where a slight runny leak drips pestilentially, like a child's runny nose, into a wet towel, a rancid odor of rot emanating from it.

"Why don't you have the leak fixed? Call the landlord. You're so apathetic."

"I can't. The landlord deserted the building. He's not fixing anything anymore. It's going to be torn down in six months, but till then it's abandoned and I don't have to pay any more rent. Isn't that a bargain?"

"That's fantastic!"

"Come away with me."

"I can't."

He sticks his finger in my cunt. "You're wearing a diaphragm!" He's insulted. It means I don't love him enough, that I would want to plug myself up to his

130

magnificent, loving, special sperm, each of which bears a heart with his initials on it as a special emissary of love to my egg.

"I don't want a baby, Sam."

He sulks, his hands behind his head, gazing up at the ceiling. A minute later he's trying to excite me, to elicit through passion proof of my love. Believe me, I'd like to be excited too. I wonder what I'm missing. While his lips are rubbing all over my body like a hungry snail nibbling the waste products of the sea, and pressing as it moves along, I think about what he told me about his former lover on the kibbutz in Israel who is now married to a rabbi. How the moment he'd penetrate her she'd begin moaning and screaming, and he showed me how. And when one time they went visiting overnight, and he began making it with her, when he inserted his penis she just couldn't control herself and began yelling so he immediately desisted. He told me about how much she was in love with him and how much he loved those sounds, but he didn't love her, so it wasn't hard to leave her. He loves me but I don't make those noises. I feel inadequate.

I never come the first time, but since all we ever did was stay in bed, there was no urgency. The second time he could really hold out. He pounded away as if he were making chopped liver in a wooden bowl. I could feel his balls banging gently against the very insides of my thighs. One day they'd just roll off and he'd have to go looking for them under the bed. There was something about being pounded away at this way that appealed to me. I did make sounds, but mostly of the air being pressed out of me at every stroke. He'd like to pound those moans out of me by violence, evoke the feeling for him that he wanted me to have by banging it into me, and then out, like artificial respiration. I was conflicted. I wanted to spite him by not having an orgasm but I wanted at the same time to be released of the pressure of appreciating his

131

masculine performance. With all my conflicts clashing like a bad rehearsal of the Goldman Band, I came. Then I didn't feel like fucking any more and did my best to make it quick.

We lie there, bodies glowing with sweat, which drips off onto the disheveled sheet, all sorts of fluids draining out between my legs and onto a towel I've thrown there like an unpinned diaper, leaking like the wall and sweating like the pipes. I get up and run to the john, all the goo running down my legs, tickling the insides of my thighs almost to my ankles. From the john I can hear Narcissa again, nothing like she usually sounds. This cry is coming from somewhere other than her mouth, somewhere deeper. I'd say from her cunt if it wasn't plugged up, but perhaps it's just being squeezed out of her pores. It's like the porpoise I saw in Florida that spoke through a hole on top of his head. I try to picture myself making those sounds. I try so hard I almost repeat them out loud in an effort to feel what it might be like to emit them. I'd done it before with the sounds Sam's Israeli girl made when he showed me what it sounded like. It makes me horny to think of myself feeling that way, but in real life it never happens. I mop my cunt innumerable times with toilet paper until all the stickiness seems gone, then I intrude my sticky body into my sticky clothing. My T-shirt seems damp, I can hardly pull up my jeans. My hair, not merely messy, has expanded in the damp from the semblance of order I'd created all morning in my air-conditioned bathroom, to its reality, a forty-five-inch aureole of tangled waves and kinks, no two hairs traveling in the same direction, almost a physical indictment, a continuation from the inside of my head, where things were in the same condition, to the outside; so revealing that I feel the need to cover it up, hide it somehow, make it appear straighter. I can't get the comb into it, and when I do it's immediately rejected, all the teeth broken off. When I get them out

132

of my hair I try Sam's brush, which is meant for thin, balding hair, and I have no success. I feel a mess. I can practically feel the hair growing out on my legs and under my arms in this tropical temperature.

Sam is sitting in the kitchen, naked, balls gently hanging over the edge of his stool, at the counter, picking at some feta. He offers me some and I begin picking at it too, but I get the feeling that he doesn't want me to take too much. After all, his mother made it, he has no money, and a three-inch square of it has to last him all week, so I'll wait till I go home to eat.

"Let's go outside. I have to go home," I say.

He slides into his jeans like honey into a cup of hot tea, and then into the T-shirt which has a collar in a tighter weave and stands away from his head like Queen Elizabeth's ruff. A tiny slit of brown skin shows between his shirt and the top of his jeans in the back, where it has shrunken up, and for a moment, as I gaze at that tiny slit, all his sexiness is manifest in that tiny area. I stroke him gently there.

We'd always walked home, which has been the most romantic and most enjoyable part of the whole thing for me, but tonight I'm scared to go home. I can't help recalling Herb and his threats. I can't imagine what kind of state he'll be in. I dread his sadness, or his meanness, his remorse, or his revenge. In order to stall for time, we stop in a coffee shop. Now I know the meaning of "greasy spoon." The pale aqua ceiling is green with grease, which continues down the walls approximately midway, almost to a molding across the middle of the wall where the filthy wallpaper begins. Inside the molding, if one looks closely one can see the tiny feelers of roaches swaying back and forth gracefully, impatiently waiting for darkness. As soon as I'm seated, perspiration pours out of me. In the mirror across the way, my skin is pasty and pale, each freckle seems to be standing two inches in front of

133

my face. It is four hundred degrees in here, the whole place feels as if it's being used for the exhaust from all the air-conditioners in the city. I'm starving, but I order only coffee out of deference for Sam's poverty. He wants to know whether I'd feel better if he waits downstairs for me when I get home, for a few minutes, in case I need him to either come up and beat the shit out of Herb, pack my bag, take me back to his place, or call an ambulance. I tell him it's not necessary, as I make dirty coffee circle patterns on the faded, filthy Formica tabletop. Sam borrows money from me for the tip, which makes me angry. And he didn't want me to wear my diaphragm! Well, thank god I did. Shit.

He kisses me goodbye in front of my house. It's quiet on my street, not a person is in sight.

"Are you sure you don't want me to wait?"

"Yes, I'm sure." I don't look back as I run up the stairs. The hall feels cool. I unlock my door, and the supercoolness from inside enfolds me when I enter, drying off all parts of me deep and obscure, insinuatingly. I feel cleaner immediately. Herb is walking toward me from the terrace, looking strangely animalistic. His shirt is ripped clear through the middle, the panel with the buttons on it is severed from the other two sides and is hanging down. There are huge rips at both shoulders, where his bear hair curls through.

"What happened to your shirt?" I ask.

"I ripped it," he says. "I also ripped your books."

I go and look. There's only a minor mess, he ripped only two or three, mostly just ones that he did the jackets for and that the publisher gave him for nothing. I can see that, even in passion, he knows the value of things. My appetite returns full force.

"Are you hungry?" I ask, without waiting for an answer, knowing he's always hungry, as I take the two T-bone steaks from the refrigerator and begin slicing some onions and button mushrooms. I bring it all out on a dish, the two steaks, salted, and beside them,

134

sliced, lying in pale blood, glowing onions, transparent, and slices of mushroom, opaque. It's still humid out, but dark, in spite of a hazy, insistent moon, and cooler on the terrace.

Herb starts the fire with new charcoal lighter, the most virile spurt I've ever seen, from one end of the terrace to the other. Then an enormous flame and piles of rolling smoke. It begins to rain gently, sizzling on the charcoal. I sit in the air-conditioned room, relaxed, and watch Herb on the terrace in the rain turn the enormous steaks with one hand, holding his big black umbrella over himself and the barbecue with the other.

MY DEATH

It was cool in the hallway as I locked the stroller to the filthy balustrade. I considered for a moment whether it would be easier to make two trips upstairs with the contents of the stroller, and decided to try for one. I didn't like trying to make the decision of whether I preferred my bundles ripped off or the baby kidnapped, so I decided to unload everything. With the baby in my arms, I bent down, took out his blanket, bottle, and his toys, put them alongside him in one arm; then with the other hand I lifted the huge bag of groceries out by the top of the bag—balancing it gently so the whole top didn't tear off—and settled it in my other arm. The cool, musty air felt good as it dried my perspiration. One more flight, I thought. Then, at the bottom of the second flight of stairs, something happened. I broke out into a cold sweat as I felt the blood leave my head and all my extremities. My heart began beating wildly, in an incredible arrhythmia. Then I felt an explosion so large that it was audible too, a sort of light surrounded by blackness which fell down over my eyes, leaving a residue of tiny sparks sparkling at the edges, then an incomparable nausea of the whole body, a deep nausea which included even my extremities.

This is it, I thought. What I was always afraid of. Death. I'd always thought it would be a stroke—cerebral accident, as it was called. Maybe this was a heart attack, or diabetic shock, but most likely it was a large blood vessel bursting in the brain in a sort of explosion, the blood, out of its boundaries in a rush, flooding all over, rushing down over my eyes. That's what my grandmother had died of, and I always knew it would feel like that. It actually felt familiar.

When I didn't feel my heart anymore I knew I was dead, but I didn't want to drop the baby so I thought I'd just try to get upstairs, and, too, the thought of all the groceries splattered all along the hall, the ketchup spilled, broken glass, oranges falling down the stairs all the way to the front door—and what the tenant's committee would think—filled me with dismay. I made a supreme effort, and continued carrying it all upstairs. I rested the groceries against my raised knees as I unlocked the door, fully intending to lay the baby down, and then lie down myself, being dead. But as I put the baby down and saw him kicking there on the couch, I felt sudden remorse. I knew I couldn't leave him there because as soon as I actually gave up the ghost he'd probably roll off the couch and cry piteously for hours, with no one to hear him. Just as I was trying to figure out what to do with the little guy he began to cry, and I realized that it was time for him to nurse, and it would be better if I left him fed and comfortable; so I left the food in the bag and lifted my shirt, cradling the baby, who felt hot next to my cooling flesh, which must by now be way below body temperature, and wondering whether there was still milk in a dead woman's breast. The baby sucked greedily, unaware of my condition. Certain body processes must continue from inertia for a while. I burped him conscientiously, and then he shit on me, right out the edges of his Pampers. I decided not to leave him in that condition, and also I myself didn't want anyone to find me dead

137

with shit on my lap, which brought me to the whole thing of what I should wear. I looked in the mirror and I didn't look good, but I looked as I imagined I'd look after I saw my grandfather dead, though when I saw him he had more makeup than I. My face was whiter, his was the bluish-black of a heart attack. Probably one of the arterioles in my brain had burst. And I had thought that those small lapses into senility I had experienced lately were the result of too much housework. I looked white and solid, as if I were made of marble, an article rather than a person. In a lifeless state, my face was really ugly; since I wasn't really pretty, the only thing I'd had in my favor was a sort of life, some sex appeal emanating from a type of expressiveness, which, when gone, left my face frightening in its blank, sheer ugliness of form.

Just as I'm about to lie down—with great misgivings, as I watch the baby paddle about on the rug, arms and legs moving frantically, but luckily unable to move an inch in any direction except round in a circle—I realize that it's time to pick up the other two kids from school. A person can't even die here, I think as tears (where can they be welling from?) actually fill my eyes. Maybe I can get someone to pick them up for me. I've already considered calling Dave, but would he leave the store early just because his wife has died? What about when I had the baby and he made me come home two days early from the hospital because he couldn't watch the other two and didn't want to close the store, even for a day? And the time I nearly bled to death from a hemorrhaging extracted wisdom tooth and the dentist wouldn't answer his answering service, and I asked Dave to come home and watch the three kids so I could find an emergency clinic that dispensed dental treatment, and he said he couldn't leave yet because a customer was there. So do you think he'd leave in the middle of the day for a mere death? I decided to call Ruth Roth. Maybe she'd take them to her house;

138

then I wouldn't have to worry about them and Dave could pick them up when he closed his shop.

"Hello, Ruth?"

"Hi."

"Listen, Ruth, I'm dead. Could you pick up the kids for me and keep them a while till Dave picks them up?"

"I'm dead too. I was going to call you and ask you whether you could pick up Rosalee."

"I would, but I'm really dead. I mean *dead.*"

"I'm worse than dead—I have this virus. Just pick up Rosalee today, I'll do yours tomorrow."

I decided not to hassle. I got ready to pick up my two kids, plus Rosalee.

The outside of the school is sickening even when one's feeling well. I suppose it could be uglier aesthetically, but it becomes ugly when one has to go there every day for so many years, stand in the same place, and at a certain moment see mobs of kids begin pouring out, an effusive discharge, a percolating, inundating deluge, almost as if the building itself is writhing in the throes of an enormous peristalsis.

Timothy and Rosalee, in the same class, are out, running wildly around the stroller, the baby's head swiveling around in complete circles, watching them. The two kids, increasingly wild, disturb me. There's no part of me that's sympathetic with the speed of them. I become dizzy and lean on a parked car for support.

"Stop being so wild," I say, thinking to myself that it's all because Rosalee's here, which is mostly a lie.

"You're going to hurt yourselves," I warn, like an oracle. Their movements accelerate as they interweave with other children, moving in and out, spreading along the whole street—books, noise, and food flying, like a dance choreographed by my worst enemy—and sure enough, Timothy is on the pavement, on his chin. As he cries, blood drips in drops to the spot on the concrete where his chin hit, leaving a mark. Everyone crowds around, sympathetic, telling me about all the cases they knew of where a fall on the chin bone required stitches, as I stare at the split flesh hanging at the bottom of my little boy's chin. In a semistupor, I raise my ass off the royal-blue Volkswagen, whose fender fits so neatly to my body, and rummage around in my purse for something to stanch the blood. I find a diaper without too much spit-up on it. As soon as the wound is covered with the diaper, some of the people who had become vampires pull in their teeth and begin moving away again. Timothy is at last quiet as we wait for Alex. Rosalee is also subdued. It would be very pleasant except for the fact that when Alex comes out we'll have to run over to the emergency room at St. Vincent's, which, fortunately, is right across the street from the school. Who knows how much foresight went into that seeming coincidence? I see Alex, minus her usual smile.

"What's wrong?" I ask, barely having time to be interested.

No answer. This is very common. I consider taking advantage of the situation in order not to have to hear what's the matter.

"What's the matter?"

"Ggaaaoo ooooieu mmnn . . . oooiiiiffo." She's said that whole sentence without once opening her mouth, which is excellent except for the fact that I didn't understand a word.

"Timothy fell from being wild with Rosalee," I tell her, "and we have to take him to the clinic. I think he needs stitches."

"Ggooor gigo," she says with her mouth still closed.

What I'd like to do is leave the kids at David's store before I take Timo to the hospital. It's only about a block and a half out of the way. I peer under the diaper and see that the bleeding seems to have stopped, but I know he'll need sitches by the way the wound hangs open.

"Let's go," I say. We all start moving, Timo and Alex each holding one side of the stroller handle; then

I notice that Rosalee's not with us. She's standing there, fifteen feet behind us.

"Come on!" I say. My teeth are clenched. Anger or rigor mortis?

"I can't. My mommy didn't tell me to go with you."

"Well, she called me up, but by then it was too late to tell you."

"She said never to go with anybody."

"I'm Timo's mother."

"Well, I'm not going."

"Then you'll be here forever, because I'm supposed to take you."

"I don't care. I'll wait here forever for my mommy, and when she sees I'm not with you she'll come and get me."

"Your ass," I say, and I pull her as hard as I can and place her hand around the stroller handle with as much pressure as I can, as if I am gluing it there and don't want it to come off.

When we get to David's store he comes out to meet us, probably in the hope that if he gets to us first, he can deflect us from coming into the store and distract us into going home. He's wearing his sneakers and a work shirt open to the waist. His brown, slender chest, tanned and hairless, is charming, as are his gently hairy ankles, emerging from the bottoms of his shrunken slacks and flowing, unbroken by the presence of socks, into his sneakers. He glares.

"I have to leave the kids here to take Timo to the hospital. He fell in front of the school."

"Why can't you take them? You know they'll be wild here. They might break something."

"Because I think Timo needs stitches, and the other kids will be disturbing and running around and there's no place to put the stroller and the baby will breathe infected air. Aside from that, I died this afternoon. I shouldn't even be doing anything. I could lie down

141

right now and no one would be able to call me down for it."

"You always complain," he says.

I then rip the diaper from where Timo is holding it to his chin, taking advantage of the fact that David can't bear to see any injury, no matter how slight, in order to impress upon him that it's not just for nothing I'm asking him to do this favor. He looks, turns white, puts his arm across his eyes, and runs for the store. I park the stroller, stuff the pacifier in the baby's mouth, and take off in the opposite direction with Timothy. It takes a few minutes for me to get used to walking without a stroller in front of me without falling over, but when I do, it feels so good that I don't even mind going for stitches. Timo isn't crying. He wants to know whether he can have some candy.

I know where the emergency room is; I've been there before. We wait in a long line to register. Timothy is holding the diaper to his chin and eating Good & Plenty. It's our turn.

"Name," says the secretary.

"Timothy Schor."

"Timothy? That's a strange name for a woman."

"It's not for me—it's my son."

"I thought it was you, you look so terrible," she says.

"Dead people usually look bad," I say.

She looks around in a moment of panic, as if she's trying to spot a psychiatrist on duty. She decides to terminate any communication with me other than the application for treatment. I show her his chin.

"Oh, it's bad. Looks like another mouth," she says coolly.

"Fuck you," I whispered with my death breath.

"Go to the third room on your left after the large room where that sign is, and wait," she says.

We wait. My fear is that after we wait for four hours

142

or so, we'll find out that they lost the pink paper that the secretary filled out. A nurse comes in.

"Timothy Schor?"

"Yes?"

She slips a thermometer under his tongue, and times his pulse as Good & Plenty juice streams out along the sides of the thermometer and dribbles onto the diaper. We wait more. Timothy is sitting on a tiny crib, one side of which is down, and I'm holding his hand because the crib frightens him. A woman comes in with a baby. She undresses the baby in another crib. Even though it's summer, the baby has on a sweater-and-legging ski set and a light woolen bonnet, which have to be removed; then, underneath, little shoes, tights, a dress, a tiny slip, a miniscule undershirt. She undresses the baby leisurely, carefully, right down to its medals and one Pampers, weeping gently onto its belly. She folds all the clothes neatly in a pile, takes out a soft baby's hairbrush from her large pink carrying case, and begins to gently brush its almost nonexistent hair. This must be the grooming instinct, I think. As I look at Timo, I wonder why I lack it. His hair is long; it hasn't been combed for a year and a half. He has various food stains on his face which extend down over his shirt in matching and contrasting colors. His face is long, his chin sharp. I'm considering taking him home and taping his chin together myself. Waiting so long makes me angry. I'm thinking of lying down right here and now so they can say, "She died waiting for service in the emergency clinic," but I'm afraid to leave Timo at their mercy.

A doctor comes in. He says "¿Que Pasa?"

"He fell," I say.

"Let's have a look. Ugh. What happened?" he asks Timo.

"He fell on the concrete in front of the school."

"What happened, sonny?" he asks Timo.

"I fell on the concrete in front of the school."

143

"Are you trying to accuse me of child beating?" I ask.

"Cool it, lady. This must have upset you—you don't look well. Have a seat."

"I'm already sitting."

"Well, relax. I'll tell the nurse to bring you some smelling salts. I'm going to have to take a couple of stitches. You wait here."

"I want to come with him."

"I'd rather you didn't. You look so bad, you might faint."

"If I look bad, it's because I'm dead. Smelling salts and waiting here aren't going to help. You think I'm just a hysterical woman," I screamed, "but I'm not— I'm simply dead. A person could die waiting here!" I shrieked, filling the halls with my mausoleum, Creature-Feature scream. The doctor ran from the room. A minute later a nurse came back and took Timo out. The coward is probably waiting, trembling in the sewing room. Where did the doctor learn to sew? In Home Economics? Will they bring back my child? Maybe they'll take me upstairs to the loony section. There's no need to fear that—loony space is at a premium these days. If you really go insane bad, you have to check in at Bellevue and wait for an opening here. It's the Concord of mental hospitals. And on the wall, to minimize my sufferings is a crucifix, a painted metal Christ on a wooden cross: passive, limp, blood painted with a metallic glow streaming from every nail wound. Actually he's beyond suffering. As depicted here, he must already be dead. They bring in Timo, with shiny dried tear rivulets and a stretched mouth.

At the cashier's I say, "How much is it?"

"Sixteen dollars for a visit to the emergency room plus four stitches at ten dollars a stitch—that's forty plus sixteen—plus the X-rays that they took to see whether the bone was chipped and the entire-body X-rays they took to see whether he showed signs of previous child battering."

144

"You expect me to pay for the unauthorized X-rays that you took for your own use, having nothing to do with my child's injury? You get a special grant for that! I should sue you for exposing him to unnecessary X-rays!

"Lady, I didn't take the X-rays, so don't say 'you.' I'm only the cashier."

"Just send me a bill, I don't carry that much money—even Rockefeller doesn't. He has credit cards. Do you accept credit? How about BankAmericard?" She hid under the desk.

As we walk away, I get a glimpse of red carpet and scarlet armchairs, matching the red costume in the portrait of the Cardinal that's hanging above the chairs. Incredible interior, I think, planning to return someday and shoot it with color film. I feel genuine regret when I realize that I'll never be back to shoot anything. I'll be lucky if I can lie down before I decompose. But who shall I leave my Minolta Autocord to? Let David keep it all, even though he prefers 35mm.

"Where were you for so long?" asks Dave when we return to the store. Does he think we lied to him in order to go see a movie or something? "How much did it cost?" he asks.

"I'm not sure—they want to charge for X-rays I didn't tell them to do."

"Well, you'll have to pay out of the household money, since it was all due to your neglect."

I held Timothy to me and wept into his bandage.

"Don't get it wet," Timo says.

On the way home the baby begins to cry. I buy some milk, not knowing when a dead woman's milk gives out. I recall photos I've seen in *Life* and *Look* of dead Indian women, starved to death, with emaciated babies at the breast, but I never could tell whether they were still sucking. Or if they were, were they getting anything? At home, baby at my breast, I see I was wise

145

to buy the milk. After a few sucks, he cries, tries again, screams. I make a bottle. The best way to wean someone from you is to die.. Alex still looks unhappy. I asked her what's the matter; she gives me a pathetic look and bares her teeth. There's nothing there. She has no front teeth anymore. And they can't have just fallen out—on the contrary, new, permanent ones have just grown in, just achieved their full growth within the past week or two. And since they were enormous, it isn't hard to miss them now.

"What happened," I say. I don't yell.

Her face turns into a prune and tears run like streams in and out of creases and into her mouth.

"Why are you crying?"

"Because I thought you were going to yell."

Well, to tell you the truth, I feel like yelling, I feel like screaming, but it's really stupid to yell at a kid because her teeth are knocked out. And they aren't completely knocked out, just chipped off almost to the top. A good dentist could cap them.

Actually, I had thought that when David finally came home he'd take over, so that I could just die normally. It isn't so much that I wanted to die, but being already dead, I had no choice—there was something compelling about lying down. I did have dinner ready for him so that things wouldn't be too much of a strain. I also prepared food for the next four days, cold things, and wrapped them and labeled them with instructions for warming or serving or eating.

When he came in he looked at me for a minute and said, "You don't look well."

I said, "Well, it's because I'm dead, and usually dead people aren't well."

"Don't be so sarcastic," he said. "You always complain. Think of something more positive. For instance, at least you can't get cancer now. Why don't you make some coffee to take your mind off it?"

146

"Look," I said, "I'm dead and I'm going to lie down. Make yourself some instant coffee."

"I don't like instant coffee."

"Then make yourself some regular."

"But I don't know how much coffee to put in."

I made the coffee, trying to figure out where to lie down when I finally could. The whole thing seemed so unnatural at this point. It's best to just lie down the moment you die, no matter where it is? Did that mean I should descend the hall stairs and collapse at the point where I originally died? The kids were watching *Gilligan's Island* and the baby was sleeping. I lay down on the bed and was pervaded by a gentle peace, which was shattered by David calling, "Hey, where's my dinner?" He called again. I wondered whether I was capable of ever getting up. I ignored him. Eventually he'd see that something was wrong and that I'd never be able to make his dinner again, or he'd get his own fucking dinner. He continued calling an endless number of times. Finally he came in and throttled me.

"What's wrong?" he said.

"I told you. I'm dead."

"You're just a hypochondriac. Move over." He lay down beside me—squeezed in because I didn't move over. Then he moved over on top of me.

"How can you do this to a dead person?" I was really indignant over the indignity.

"Well, I'll try. It's sort of exciting." He disembarked for one mad moment while he ripped off his clothes. Then he proceeded to rip off mine, which was more difficult, since I didn't even raise my hips so he could pull down my underpants. He sublimated himself onto my body again, kissing my limp lips and pumping into my unresponsive limbs. Obviously he wasn't enjoying it, he was spending all the time trying to arouse me.

"Why can't you move just a little?" he said. "I feel like a necrophiliac."

"If you were a necrophiliac you'd dig making it with me like this," I said. He tried some more.

147

"Oh, fuck it," he said, dismounting. "Why can't you excite me?"

"Why does your excitement depend on mine? You're insecure. You take it too personally. It's a known fact that dead people don't respond even if Paul Newman were wiggling his cock into their pubic hair."

He went to put water into the tub for his bath, which is too bad because it occurred to me to take a bath too, and I was in a hurry. I put the kids to bed. I looked in the mirror. My face was already thinner; my eyes looked like melted fish eyes. My skin was like cheese cake with birthday-candle blue lips. I heard Dave shouting from the bathroom over the sloshings of water, "Too bad I never took out insurance for you. I never dreamed you'd die so young. I'd never have to work again." I felt like weeping but not a tear came to my concave fish eye.

I rested on the toilet while I let my bath water in, nice and hot. I left my hand under the faucet, where it flipped to and fro like a seal's flippers. When the tub was full I ingressed into the water gently, insinuating my body in a bit at a time, enjoying the sensual pleasure of the extreme heat on the lower part of my body and the goose flesh on the upper, unimmersed portions. When the sensation mitigated, I rested my back against the curved back of the tub and slowly slid downward. I continued sliding down until I felt the water crawling up over my lips, feeling the water in my nose, over my eyes, and tickling my scalp as it flooded fluidly through my hair. I never bothered to come up. I noticed that the oblivion I was experiencing was not that much different from the usual.

THE LIZARD MAN

My shape is most like a cylinder, how long I don't know, sometimes I seem longer, sometimes shorter, and I am constructed of many layers of scales, or crust. Layer upon layer thickens my cylindrical form. I don't know whether the top and bottom of me is open or closed, but I can peer out through two conelike holes, or perhaps I'm just assuming they are two holes, perhaps it is one oval-shaped telescopelike hood, and I peer through from deep inside. I know I'm deep inside from the way I peer out, and there are shadows before the light. Feet I have none, because my mother always says, "At least he saves me money on shoes." I'm proud when she says that, at the same time my feelings are hurt. Inside my deeply scaled or barky exterior I have no idea how large or small I am. In fact, I don't know where I am. What I think of as a covering or container might well be me, or I might be a miniature of the shape of my mother encased like a squirrel in a hollow tree, or I might be as small and thin as a pinworm, or the nerve of a tooth. Mother always says I couldn't be hers. Probably not. I'm always fearful that she won't take care of me anymore. Sometimes she threatens to send me to the home for the retarded. Then again, my skin is more like barnacles, but softer, crustier barnacles, and even a bit greasy, like buttered

149

toast. I used to long for mom to hold me, touch me, but I sense her repulsion and disgust, so I show no more desire for affection because I'm self-conscious of the playacting that ensues. She keeps me very neat though, always changes my moist and greasy sheets once a day, but my feelings are hurt because she picks me up with a towel, which makes me think that she can't stand to touch me. She moves me over with the towel to do one side of the bed, then she picks me up with the towel over the bunched-up part of the new sheet that runs along the center of the bed, then she pulls that side over and pulls out the old sheet, then the towel, and though I assume it was clean, she puts it in the pile with the dirty sheets and rolls it over her hand and arm till she reaches a part that she wishes to touch and carries it out of the room, to where, I don't know, since I haven't been out of the room for years, and when I was, I was too young to remember. My mother always speaks of my former self. According to her, I was the most beautiful plump baby. She says I was a baby boy, but I don't think she remembers. Not only don't I know whether I am male or female, I don't know how old I am. It's difficult for me to tell, due to my dependence on my mother. I say mother even though my father is alive, because dad is squeamish of sickness and sores and blood and stuff, so I haven't seen him in years. Mother told me he would be in to explain why he couldn't see me, but he kept putting it off because it was unpleasant for him. It often worries me about how I urinate and get rid of wastes, since I'm never out of my room, and furthermore, as much as my cylindrical shape allows exploration, I've never even, by gently rolling against the sheets in order to feel a sensation of a raised organ, found any outlet for urine or anything else, and must assume that they are just excreted by my whole body. That would explain the moisture on the sheets. As far as sex, probably this is how it feels to be a female, just the vague sensation of a great stream running from her. The thought

150

of that great stream excites me. I feel a vague, strange, tiny sensation localized deep inside, probably some- where on the tiny worm that is me. I don't know what to do with it. I long to touch the sensation, explore it, feel it out, find out where it is more, less, the most. I begin to thrash on my bed, throwing myself around and around in order to press my stimulated area against something, in vain, then the failure and the violence of my attempts excites me even more, until all of a sudden the bedsprings cry in a' vibrating, convulsive staccato, and knowing not what happened, I'm relaxed. I scorn thinking of the things that titillated me before. For some reason, my wonderful mother is upset and disgusted by the sound of those bedsprings. This last time I heard her cry out in anguish. "It's too much, we will have to put him somewhere, he's really so disgusting." Then dad answered, "Where can we put something as disgusting as he is?"

"Perhaps we should consult a doctor. It would be worth the fee if we can place him in a hospital somewhere. I can't even bear to change his sheets anymore."

"I don't know; I'm really ashamed for anyone to see him, and I don't trust doctors. They'll treat Robert for months, charge loads of money, then say that's the best they can do," said dad.

"What about a chiropractor?"

"I think they work on the spine and I don't know whether Robert has one. I don't believe in them anyway, because the American Medical Association doesn't endorse them."

"I'll call Iris and ask her to recommend her doctor."

About ten minutes later I heard father ask mother what Iris said.

"She said, 'Certainly not. I wouldn't want him to find out that I have a freak like that in the family. Why don't you find your own doctor and leave me out of this," and I said, 'But I won't even tell him who you are,' and she said, 'But he might find out. I've tried for years to ignore the fact that you have that Robert

151

in that room, but you insist upon talking about him, and now you want to encroach upon my life and my doctor. It's just too impossible.' "

"Why don't you just call the doctor who lives on our street?"

About ten minutes later I heard my mother weeping.

"What happened?"

"I said, 'No, it's about my son. It would really be impossible to bring him. Could the doctor come over here?' She said, 'I'm sorry, the doctor doesn't make house calls,' so I said, 'This is an emergency,' so she said, 'The doctor is totally unable to make house calls,' so I said, 'But in that case could you recommend someone who could?' so she said, 'I'm sorry, I don't know of anyone who makes house calls. Try calling the AMA; they can recommend someone who will do house calls.' Then I called the number she gave me and I said, 'I'd like the name of a doctor who will come to the house, please,' and she said, 'What do you mean, come to the house?' so I said, 'I mean I can't go out.' She said, 'One moment, please, I'll connect you with someone who has a list.' Then I waited so long I thought we were disconnected, you could die before you could get any help in this country, then someone said, 'Hold on, please,' again. A few minutes later I said, 'Hello,' and someone said, 'Can I help you?' I said, 'I'd like the name of a doctor who will come to the house,' so she said, 'One moment, please. I'll connect you with someone who has a list.' 'But,' I said, 'I'm the one who just called before. Listen,' I shouted, 'all I need is the name of a doctor who will make house calls, because my son is ill and I can't take him out.' Then she said, 'What's wrong with him? You know, nowadays even with a very high fever it's not considered dangerous to bring the child out.' I said, 'Take my word for it, I can't bring him out.' 'Okay, I have a list of doctors who'll come to your house in an emergency. Dr. Gormely, 989-2437, and Dr. Rubin, 679-4379,' so I said, 'That's it? Just two?'

152

and she said, 'That's it. How many doctors do you need?' I called the first, Dr. Gormely. I said, 'Dr. Gormely was recommended by the AMA as a doctor who comes to the house if need be,' so the person who answered said, 'And where are you located?' So I said, 'Seventeen-seventy-six East ᴸThirteenth Street,' and she said, 'Oh, I'm sorry, the doctor only makes calls within a radius of five hundred feet of his office, so I'm afraid you're out of his district.' "

My mother burst into tears. Daddy said, "Listen, it's not so bad. We'll wrap him up and take him over."

Mother came into my room, her arms full of towels. She laid an ugly striped hand towel beside me on the bed, then she picked me up with another towel and laid me on the striped one, then she placed a large bath towel with a picture of a naked woman getting out of the bath on it, and placed me, wrapped in the other towels, right on the lady and closed it around me. I was extremely aroused, but I decided to wait until she left the room before I did anything about it. After a few minutes, I could see that she wasn't going to leave the room without me, and all the while she was sniffing frantically to keep her nose from running on me while she was preparing me.

"Where are we going?" I asked.

"We're going to the doctor."

"Why," asked I, "am I sick?" My dear mother looked up, and I saw her for a moment totally disarmed and unself-conscious, her thin lips kissing each other in desperation.

"No, maybe the doctor can find out what's wrong with you and make you better, beautiful as you were before, and make you look like the rest of us again."

I was pleased that she closed the whole bath blanket around me. Though I would have liked to see my dad again, I was quite preoccupied with the thought that the woman on the bath blanket was actually wrapped around me and I wondered in what direction, up and down or across. I was absolutely sure that her musty

153

cunt was over my face and I could imagine looking straight up into it and discovering new worlds, or imagine an extension, if I had one, something like a tongue, only longer, darting straight up and all the time her terrycloth body holding me around, warming me and absorbing all my excretions.

After a totally exciting journey, jogging in the body of my beloved, jerking and joyfully jumping, just about to shake my last shake, mother stops moving. I give one last hop of my own—she's not going to frustrate me again. I've almost hopped right out of her arms. Someone says, "Won't you please sit down?" She moves me to the side as I feel her body squatting.

"Please don't make me hold him," whispers my father. Mother makes her special clicking sound with her tongue that expresses annoyance and holds me tight to her. It's too hot in here and I can't breathe, the stupid woman must be blocking my air. I try to decide whether to imagine that the terrycloth girl is smothering me with her breast or belly and try to get excited again, or whether I'd better flip about and try to communicate the fact that every minute I am losing oxygen, and if mother wants to kill me that way she could have done it at home. The nurse asks her if she's like to open the blanket. She insists upon calling the towel a blanket. She tries to explain to mother that if I have a fever it'll become worse if I'm wrapped so warmly in a hot place. My mother's panic and the towel make her suspicious.

"Is he bleeding?" she queries. "If so, the doctor would take you right away, as soon as I fill out a record sheet for him."

"No, that's not what's wrong," said mother, dooming me to a death by smothering.

"Let me see the little guy," pleads the nurse. My mother slips the top of the towel down and parts the top, spreading it with her thumb and forefinger, which excites me the most as I imagine her spreading two

154

terrycloth labia, but I'm almost sucked out of mother's arms by the deep inhalation of the nurse as she spots only a tiny portion of me and a bit of the part I see through must be exposed, for it takes a moment for what I see to be registered: two large nostrils full of black hair and a protruding upper lip.

"How did that happen?" asks the nurse in matter-of-fact tones. "Why didn't you bring him sooner?"

"We did have him to the doctor once when he was still a baby and the sores began, but the doctor said he doubted whether he could cure it. He thought it was progressive but perhaps after a while would go away by itself. We've been waiting twenty-three years and it doesn't look any better."

"Put him down over there while we do the chart. Please cover him again—that old lady over there has a bad heart."

Mother says, "I hope I didn't trouble you any by bringing him."

"It's no trouble at all. The fee for the first visit is twenty-five dollars, and only ten dollars each subsequent visit. Any tests and immunizations are extra. Child's age?"

"Thirty-five."

"Ever been hospitalized, had any surgery?"

"No."

"Anyone in the family have diabetes, cancer? Any mental illness, any Mongolism, cretinism, retardation? Chicken pox? Measles? Mumps?"

"If he had had chicken pox or measles I wouldn't have been able to tell."

"Well, what shall I say, yes or no?"

"Can't you say maybe?"

"I don't know, let me ask the doctor."

Mother comes over and picks me up. I've secreted so much from the heat and the terrycloth girl, terrycloth love, I almost slip right out of the towel, but mom catches me and we go into another room, where, at the request of the doctor, she unwraps me—too quickly,

155

I fear, for suddenly, I'm in the light, piercingly white. I hear the doctor give his professional opinion.

"Ooohhh, ughhh, what on earth is that? How disgusting!" He jabs me gingerly with his forefinger, which he immediately washes. Then he searches about in a large autoclave but can't find what he needs. He unwraps two ice-cream-pop sticks and tries to move me with one in each hand, attempting to lift me with both of them, and I slip down onto the paper-covered table, which really jars me and makes me angry so I tell him in my hollow voice to go fuck himself. For the first time he smiles. "Nurse, come here a moment." He tries again to lift me while the nurse stands by expectantly.

She says, "How revolting." My mother and father stand weakly by, unwilling to come to my defense, so from the opening in me I tell them to keep their professional opinions to themselves. The doctor laughs. The nurse says, "Very cute, but I'm going back to my desk or I won't be able to eat my lunch." That would be the best thing for her, because when she is standing the bottom part of her looks as if it belongs to another person, a shorter person who is three times fatter than the top person. Her breasts look interesting, but one can hardly make them out in that insipid white uniform. If I had the chance to design nurses' uniforms, I could really do something with them.

But I can hardly think with the doctor trying to pry me onto my side with those damn sticks. He finally picks up large metal calipers, tries to grip me with them to lift me and see my underside. He looks at the greasy excretions on the towel.

My mother says, "What do you think?"

"I'm going to take some tests. I can't say right off what he has; it's possibly an allergy or a nervous disease, but again, I can't offer any hope of a cure since he seems totally absorbed by whatever he has, at this point."

"Then what's the point of the tests?" asks my mother.

156

"To find out what he has. There's always the possibility of a cure, or at least an alleviation." He gets a long, flat piece of glass, then takes a few ice-cream-pop sticks and with one he scrapes some excreta off the towel and smears it on the glass, then he scrapes my crust near the top of me and smears it on the glass. He does the same with various parts of me. I'm becoming very bored, but he's nearing an area that seems to be stimulated by those long wooden sticks. I turn my body this way and that in order to get the stick to the right spot, and all of a sudden the rat is finished. He makes a note of something.

"I'm going to do a blood test," he says. I am planning to roll over, off the table under the small table that the autoclave is on, but mother grabs me in time and I thrash around, this time in fear. The needle is poised for a moment as the doctor tries to decide where to put it. He inserts it into one of the barnaclelike crusts about one third of the way down on my cylindrical body, and begins drawing something out, a watery-looking fluid which, when it achieves a certain volume, becomes a bit greenish. When he sees this the doctor is confused and looks as if he wonders whether to bother finishing, but he does. He tells mother to dress me and come into his consultation room. The nurse comes in right on time to roll down clean paper on the table. For the operation of ripping off the part I had just used, she puts on a transparent glove, which makes her hand look like an udder, which I just long to suck.

"The results will be ready in a few days, but I can't really offer any hope."

"If there's no hope, Doctor," cries mother, "what can I do with him? His father and I can't take much more. He needs constant physical care, it's worse than having an invalid or an infant around, and when hope is gone . . . of his being normal again . . . I mean, it's all so useless."

"Look, I understand your problem. Do you have a

157

medical plan, Blue Cross, HIP, GHI? No? Then you won't be able to get one now for him, only for the other members of the family who are well."

"That doesn't seem fair," says my father.

"Do you have Medicaid?—though it doesn't cover my fee. Apply for Medicaid tomorrow and I'll try to get him into a hospital. Otherwise there are alternatives. You could put him into a foundling home, but they might not take someone that ill. It would be against the law to abandon him. I could try to get him into an old-age home, but I have a thought. It occurs to me that the best place for your boy would be a freak show. There he could lead a normal life with freaks just like himself, and provide for himself at the same time, giving himself some sense of accomplishment. Your best bet would be the freak show."

"The freak show!" mother screams. "Are you intimating that my boy is a freak?"

"No, I'm not, Mrs. Perkis, but be practical. He's not legally an orphan, an elderly, a cretin, yet you wish to get him placed somewhere so that you both can have a good life."

"I'm sorry," says mother. "You're right. I'll try to get Medicaid first, and if that doesn't work I'll see about the freak show."

I won't allow her to get rid of me like that. But actually I'm in a hopeless dependent position. On the way home mother's crying because father's not carrying me, but is expounding one of his favorite theories that you can get the best sandwiches at bars. Mother just sniffles. She's heard all that before, as have I. At least in one thing do I feel on mother's side: in moments like this, when we realize we can't depend on dad for anything. But essentially she still prefers him to me.

"A freak show," she weeps.

"Why don't we go over to the freak show," father suggests, "and see what it's all about. Maybe he'll be very happy there. Maybe he can send some money home every week."

"You're kidding," she screams, "you mercenary fiend."

"You don't care whether he's happy," father says, "you just don't want a son who's a freak. Why shouldn't he pay back some of the money we've expended on him while he just lies there like a vegetable? I've figured out that from the time of his birth, counting hospital expenses, he's already cost me thirty thousand dollars, and if I count the loss to me of your salary all these years that you couldn't work but had to stay home and care for him, it would run into a hundred thousand. What's the difference between a home for cretins or a freak show?"

"One is so base, so degenerate." As I have never seen a freak show, mother's attitude influenced me against it immediately. It even instilled a fear that made me unable to concentrate on the terrycloth woman I was wrapped up in. But I had confidence that mother would protect and defend me from anything ugly.

My clean sheet felt wonderful to me as mom rolled me out of it at home. I begged her to leave the towel with the terrycloth girl on it, but she insisted that it had to be washed first. She promised to bring it back. The next day I asked for it but she said she had other things to do besides wash towels. Then I saw it. Just the corner, white, a tiny bit of flesh-colored ankle, and another bit of black open-toe and heel shoe, the heel so thin and black you could kill a vampire with it. Then it disappeared, then a little more, a bit of the leg and other foot, then gone, then nothing but the other side of the towel entirely, enticingly. I realized that it was hanging on the line, drying. It'd been washed and this was probably the last I would see of my terrycloth girl, for some reason of mother's. Jealousy, perhaps. But I was becoming extremely excited by these teasingly tiny glimpses of my favorite. Why had mother lied to me about having washed my towel? I couldn't think anymore. With each gust of wind I saw more and more of my beloved, a ridiculously tiny waist, part of a breast! . . . then suddenly nothing for a while. This was absolutely the most frustratingly exciting thing I had ever experienced. I tried to prolong this joy, but to no avail; my body turned and trembled in spite of myself. I lay still, totally relaxed, while the bed springs continued to squeak.

With the doctor's help, mother got me an appointment to have an interview at a home for Mongoloid children. So, wrapped in clean towels, with no pictures this time, I'm unwrapped on the floor of a large office. Halfway up the room on all sides are walls of glass. I see a ridiculous woman looking down at me. She questions the fact that I'm the correct Mongoloid for whom the appointment for the interview was made. A quick call to the doctor corroborates that fact.

"Has he ever been institutionalized?" asked the woman. Mother was about to pick me up and take me over to the desk, but the woman said it would be just as well to leave me over there, as I would be tested after my interview. She clears her throat in a corny way. I know she's probably attracted to me. Perhaps she thinks of me as a live human dildo, and can't bear close proximity to me. Mother warned me to behave. If I don't pass the Mongoloid test, she told me, it's the freak show for me! The dreaded freak show. I lie there, trying to be still, at the same time trying to look up her legs, as I see a glimpse of dark hair on the thigh . . . a beginning of pubic hair? I should like to follow that tiny course of fur to its thickest. It excites me, this enforced stillness while making this discovery. It was purely up to her now, and how she moved. She was asking questions in her deep voice, every once in a while leaning over to look down mother's dress. The doctor had told her exactly what to say.

Had my mental capacities ever been tested? "No."

What was my religion? "Jewish."

What were my physical capabilities? Were there other Mongoloids in my family? Not that mother knew of.

160

"It might go better for you if you have," said the interviewer.

"I'm sorry." Mother blushed. "I can't think of any offhand."

"Okay," shrugged the woman, her broad shoulders obliterating her stocky neck. I was sure she was a Taurus. I was concentrating so hard on trying to catch a glimpse of something up her skirt that I wasn't aware of her voice, even though afterward I recall that she must have been questioning me, but I was too involved to answer.

"The inattentive syndrome," she told mother. She crossed her legs and I caught my breath. It was so sudden, like a gift, after so much waiting. Unfortunately, she had underpants on, though some grass spurted out over the edges and grew down her leg in a very provocative way. I imagined her cunt, hanging slightly with age, hairy, flesh loose. I lay still—mother had warned me—yet I didn't want to stay in a school for Mongoloids. I didn't like this woman enough, and who knows whether those Mongoloids would appeal to me. Mother and the woman were leaving me alone in this room. She looked down at me and the whistle at her neck swung out first, then her breasts, then the keys at her hips.

"We're going to leave you for a while. You play with some of the toys here, dear." She ushered mother out.

I lay still for a moment, enjoying the silence, when a moment later I saw them both reappear, outside the room, peering through the glass on one side. I looked around and saw two men and one woman looking through the glass on the other side. They were apparently waiting for me to do something. Well, I would, if I could find anything stimulating among this mess of child-guidance junk, but looking around this room, decorated in primary colors, I couldn't find anything the least bit lecherous. All I did was lie there and look around. Doubtless no one could see me looking out through my crusty shield from deep within. I sought

161

something among those primary colors, secondary, tertiary, and plain varnished nontoxic wood. I noticed that they were all taking notes except for mother. I believe that head woman desired mother, unless those glances that she gave, those sidelong looks, were because, while the white-coated ones were taking notes on me, she was taking notes on mother and the woman on the other side was taking notes on the head woman, all to be discussed at various staff and board meetings, determining status and abilities, but when I saw the way unconsciously and delectably that person rolled her moist tongue around the top of a pencil, while cogitating for a second here and there, like a snake around a vine, something swelled within to a point where it would burst if something weren't done about it, and I rolled around on the moist towel in oblivious ecstasy, unaware of white coats, doctors, mother, all but that entwining tongue tip, volatile mobile wet pink slightly textured, but alive by itself. At this moment she was not even aware that it was moving gently and seductively over the top of a pencil, causing the rolling and writhing that a loglike shape like mine could perform and which was the very thing that was absorbing her. The give-and-take of this relationship thrilled me until finally it all burst. In a state of apathetic boredom, I wished that the interview were over and that mother would come and retrieve me. The woman in charge watched with curiosity while mother wrapped me in my towel considerably stained with excreta, probably still fascinated by my resemblance to a dildo. The next day mother received notification that I was not accepted to the school for Mongoloids as I didn't appear to have the nature of a true Mongoloid, aside from physical characteristics, an area in which they were willing to be flexible, if I had shown the proper behavioral requirements.

Mother cried on the phone with Dr. Rubin, and he suggested that we go over to the hospital and at least be interviewed while waiting for the Medicaid to come through. Mother, becoming extravagant at the hope of possible release from her lifetime burden, embraced me in a floral royal-blue towel, the trellis of Spanish design, making me feel quite dashing. The fringes that ensconced the edges were in just the right places, being softly and mildly stimulating, enough to make my trip on the crowded bus bearable. If mother would only tilt me forward and down just a bit, the soft and gentle pressure of the fringe would be intensified ever so slightly; but just at the right moment, mother is rising from our vibrating, jolting, delightfully bumping bus seat, me in her arms, and is delicately wending her way, while the bus is still in motion, to the door. She nearly falls down the steps and bangs me against the handle of the door. Fuming with rage and indignation, I begin to flip about in mother's arms in a tantrum the likes of which I barely remember, when she whispers, "It's the freak show for you!" Instantly I'm frozen. Though I've never seen the freak show, I can tell by her voice that it's a repulsive place, so I calm down.

After waiting at the hospital cashier's desk for a half hour, we are told that we have to take a number off a pile of numbers on ocher cardboard that sits on a little shelf behind a glass partition. Mother looks at her number with all the hope of a bingo player whose card is almost full: it's number fifty-three. The cashier is in a cage, pushing the keys of the cash register like an orangutan giving a concert at Carnegie Hall. Each of her hands is like a group of cocktail franks, the bluish white of the underside of her arm hangs down loosely, flaps with motion and vibrates in a fascinating way as she pushes the keys, like trembling waves of jelly, the vibration, then the ripples, then a new vibration, strengthening the ripples, causing a new set. Her voice suddenly gave a meaning to mother's arbitrary number fifty-three, by placing it in space, as she calls, "Number fourteen." In nervous exasperation, mother sought a seat and prepared to wait. Eventually the cashier called our number. Mother jumped up, making a quick contact between the fringes and a most sensitive spot that I had been concentrating on all along, causing a surprise culmination of all those carefully stored and growing sensations, combined with the sensation of disappointment at mother's getting up at the wrong moment, which turned out to be the right moment combined with the right movement. When mother handed the cashier a five-dollar bill, she said, "There's a sign here that says we can't cash anything over a dollar."

"But the clinic costs four and I'm giving you a five, all you have to do is give me one and we're even."

"I'm sorry," said the cashier, "you can see the sign, that's the rule."

"Well they're stupid rules," cries mother. She places me on the floor right where she's standing, in fear of losing her place, but the cashier calls the next number and all goes on without us. I'm going to help mother by shaking loose of my towel and looking repulsive, but someone has noticed mother's plight and holds out five singles. Mother grabs them, gratefully crumbling her five into his other outstretched hand. "Thanks." She slips behind the person at the cashier now and smiles, anxious not to alienate the cashier, who at this point wields power.

"Where is your clinic card?" asks the cashier.

"Clinic card?"

"Have you been registered for the clinic here?"

"No," says mother.

"Go to room 107 C and then come back here." She points and we follow her finger docilely, but there is a large line plus a benchful of people in front of 107 A, B, and C, and only Miss Bierman to handle it all. Mother props herself against the wall, me in her arms, resignedly, but her fat face is flushed with a mixture of anger and self-pity.

"If it weren't for your father, we wouldn't be forced to endure this awful treatment," she whines into me. Once again, I don't defend father because I have a

164

need for affection, and this temporary collusion with mother is very satisfying. It doesn't even bother me that the main reason for banishing me to my room, besides shame, was so that I wouldn't stain her new carpeting in the living room. In fact, I can trace my final banishment to that time when she was on the point of a nervous breakdown from caring for me and father told her that she could spend all the money that they had been saving for a vacation on new living-room furniture and carpeting. She spent days poring over furniture catalogs and her renewed interest in something revived her spirit, even though I was banished and the door closed.

Miss Bierman is ready for us with a nod and a smile. Mother sits down at a desk while she fills out the usual questionnaire.

"Thirty-five years old," she says as her eyes look upon my crusts with curiosity. "Was he born like that?"

"Oh, no," says mother, "he was a beautiful baby."

"I was going to suggest the freak show, but perhaps he can be cured, though I don't see how he can get his arms and legs back."

Mother starts to cry. "That's what my husband says, because he wants me to get rid of him right away. Then I have to go through all these interviews and examinations and questions and he doesn't have to have anything to do with him. He hadn't even seen his son in twenty-five years, until last week."

"Men!" says Miss Bierman. We take our salmon-colored booklet with my clinic number on it and the admonition that if we lose or bend it or get it sloppy in other ways we'll be made to pay ten cents for a new one. Mother's been carting me around for hours and doesn't know where to put the clinic booklet till we get back to the cashier, and is deathly afraid to get it stained by slipping it in my towel for a moment, so she carries it to the cashier in her teeth. Her face flushed salmon also, my mother's little brown eyes plead, Please don't make me take another number.

165

She gets behind the person at the cage, makes herself unobtrusive until it's her turn.

"What clinic are you going to?"

"Dermatology," says mother.

"No, you have to be referred to dermatology clinic."

"Regular medical, then."

"There is no regular clinic this morning; you'll have to come back at one o'clock."

Mother still has the salmon booklet in her mouth, her words have been sneaking out around it through the clenched teeth. "Well, we came very far," she says, "and you can see he really has a skin problem. Can't we just see the dermatologist?"

"I'm sorry, those are the rules."

I'm falling through space only for an instant before I'm smashed against the aqua wall under the cashier's bars by the pressure of mother's girdle, as her hand pushes through the bars and grabs the cashier by her permanent. She pulls the head back and forth by those curls, the red mouth pursed in surprise like an anus between her rotund white cheeks. The enormous cashier emerges from behind her cage and she and mother are rolling on the floor, mother's false teeth caught on the cashier's arm, which she is clutching in pain, while her other hand is engaged in mother's nostrils. Women fight funny, I think as I try desperately to roll out of the way, since if either of those bodies rolls over me, instant death is certain, though rolling is almost an impossibility while wrapped in a limp Turkish towel with heavy fringes. But I manage by sheer will, plus an acceleration of movement, to turn at least forty-five degrees in the other direction while the cashier's body is entirely on top of mother's, the teeth still clamping the flesh of her upper arm, vibrating while she straddles mother, who is gently splayed out around them both like a frame while being pressed between the cashier and the institution linoleum. I am, in the meantime, trying to get a glimpse of something up the cashier's skirt, which she makes no attempt

166

to pull down and is slowly crawling higher with each movement of the struggle and finally is at the tops of her elastic stockings, when all I see after the legs emerge from the tight stockings is a veritable explosion of white flesh bursting from the stockings in one mass, both legs merging at that point like mashed potatoes. It did excite me a bit to see her on top of mother like that, until the guard came and pulled the cashier off. Mother was told to leave immediately, but wouldn't go without her teeth, which were still hanging from the cashier's arm. Mom retrieved me from the floor.

Tears streamed from her eyes all the way home on the bus, flowed from the reddened edges of her small, brown, lashless eyes, dripping out from under her harlequin eyeglass frames with the marcasite corners, and right down her cheeks onto my towel. As soon as we debark from the bus, salty rivulets on mother's cheeks, a deep chill shoots through my body like a sharp unbearable pain and I feel the lack of arms to throw around myself, causing the pain to feel even sharper, then another chill rolling upon me like waves of the ocean, and suddenly the nerve which must be my inner body, my me, is trembling uncontrollably and painfully and I can't even speak, just hope that such violent shivering reverberates enough to indicate to mother my need to be rushed home and barraged with blankets, enfolded, enwrapped in their beautiful and magnificent warmth. Mother's hurrying, dear mother, she's as anxious to get home as I am, her fat body hurrying as fast as she's able, her ankle turning now and then, but not stopping her for a moment. Could it be on my account that mother hurries so? Dear mother, do you really care for ugly me? She fumbles to open the door. Father's home waiting, but he will not open the door for us, even though I'm precariously hanging off mother's arm, my wet towels dragging dangerously on the floor, for fear of seeing and being disgusted by the sight of me, which might impair the pleasurable consumption of his dinner.

167

Mother rushes me to my room. She remembers to get a clean towel to put on the bed and leaves me lying there with my painful internal shivering and trembling and not a blanket or even a towel to cover me with.

"How did it go?" father says.

"It's impossible," says mother. "I just can't go through with it again." She's changing her clothes, washing her face—she's forgotten to close the bedroom door all the way, I catch glimpses of her in her corset and stockings, a sight which in ordinary circumstances would have interested me, to say the least, but at the moment, all my paroxysms having ceased, I'm lying there totally indifferent to all, totally washed out. . Mother's combing her hair and putting on fresh make-up, while father tells her how when he called the Medicaid office, after getting a busy signal for an hour, they told him that because the nature of our case was so unusual the information was repeatedly rejected by the computer, barfed out time and again, until finally even father's copy of his income tax had been lost and it would all have to be redone for a reapplication.

I heard their voices faintly in my weak drowsiness. Cold as I'd been before, I was dry and hot now, each crusty crater of mine sinking deeper and drier. I heard father promise that it would all end and they would take me to the freak show tomorrow and leave me there. Mother burst into tears at the finality of her own decision, expressed so directly in father's weak voice.

"It's so degrading," she wept over and over again. My dry tears burned my whole body in an unsuccessful attempt to emerge from some orifice. I'd thought mother was especially close today. How I needed her love. And now, total abandonment to the hated place. After another unsuccessful attempt at crying, I decided I'd make one last attempt to salvage myself from degradation. Burning hot and weak, my breathing dry and raspy, I planned to roll myself from the bed and under the radiator, which would be my target and hiding

168

place until death should overcome me. I'm feeling a bit better after mother's fed me some tea. She can tell I'm hot even without touching me. She looks in Dr. Spock to see what I have. It's either croup or pneumonia. It says to give me an enema or a rubdown for the high fever. She can't decide which to do. She brings in the syringe, but, turning me over with a corner of the towel, she can't figure out where to stick the nozzle. She finishes feeding me my tea, and although she's crying again, the tears forced to flow down the salty riverbed of former tears, she doesn't really seem concerned for me. On the contrary, she's anxious to get out of the room, she's spilling tea everywhere, she's separated herself from me already and is anxious to be rid of my physical presence.

In the gray light of dusk, the air filling gradually with particles of darkness except for a soft last glow, I angle myself correctly for my final roll under the radiator, and for most of the night, to mother's sobs and father's snores, I try to gain the impetus to roll myself right off the bed and by sheer inertia reach the radiator, which I am hoping to fit under without any of me showing along the edges. After endless attempts I finally roll, then stop. I'm at my destination, safely under the radiator, but strangely enough I no longer care about that or anything else. I can't even muster the energy to try to feel for the edge of the radiator to see whether all of me is under. I'm lulled to sleep by the sound and effort of my own breathing.

I hear mother in my room. She's yelling to father to help her look for me, which he won't do just in case he should find me.

"I can't think where he could be, since he can't walk," she says. She repeatedly looks in the same places, the only ones she can imagine my getting to, and then other quite impossible places, like in her drawers and her jewelry box, she rustles her beads, then is back to looking under the bed. I'm feeling quite ill but very pleased with myself, when it becomes

169

clear to me that mother is actually giving up the search, believing that finding me is an impossibility, and unrealistically pleased at my disappearance, thereby preserving her from a more maudlin separation: the freak show. In disbelief that she would give up her search for me, I panic and find myself seeking a way to attract her attention before she leaves the room. I try to groan miserably, but no sound is emitted. Mother is leaving the room—for heaven knows how long. Finally a small croak emerges, then another, and mother finds me, dried and dusty.

"Just like the time we lost the turtle," she tells father.

"Is he okay?"

"He appears to still be ill. I'll moisten him a bit. It did the turtle a world of good. Then we'll leave." She splashes some cold water over me, then leaves me enveloped in nothing but chills until she finishes putting on her makeup. Then she wraps me in an old worn towel, my last towel, and one she knows she'll never see again. She arranges it so that most of the holes are covered with other parts of the towel, but it's too late to warm me now. I don't care whether I live or die.

I am just barely conscious when we reach the freak show. There is a semicircular entranceway covered with life-size paintings from top to bottom and going all around, of the most fantastic creatures I'd seen. It had an aura of funky sensuality, a decadence that was very exciting to me. There were lights all around and a small platform in the center of the semicircle where a man in purple pants and a red satin shirt open to the waist was calling people to see Lisa the Snakeskin Girl, Sondra and Sara the Siamese Twins, Don the Donkey Boy, Pearl the Boneless Lady. The fire-eater and four girls were on the platform, with beautiful bodies and long hair and almost nothing on, dancing and twirling and—would you believe it, folks?— they're really men.

170

"Lady, what can I do for you?"

Mother held me up in my old towel.

"Beautiful, beautiful. The most authentic thing I've ever seen." Everyone gathers around. "How great, he's the most disgusting thing, a real freak."

I was sick, but they all took good care of me. They are all friendly and loving people. They haven't decided whether to call me the Bark Boy, Lizard Man, or Log Lad, but when they do I will have my portrait painted for the front outside. Most loving is Pearl the Boneless Lady, whose body is as soft as pillows and cushions my crusts, whose torso is like a pillow balanced on two pillow legs with two pillow breasts and two pillow arms with little tiny minipillow fingers—three on each arm, and a soft soft pillow head balanced on her pillow torso, and her soft pillow body, only eighteen inches high while standing, caresses me and spreads its softness around me, while those three minipillow fingers of each hand search and search and caress inside every crusty crater of my body, ferreting out sensation after sensation. No longer do I have to roll frantically and ferociously seeking my own satisfaction. While she caresses my craters she shows me hidden pillow wonders under her skirt, which she gently lifts with other pillow fingers one and two and three at a time, and I see pillow lips. Here I'm immersed in love, well cared for, happy, and useful. I can't figure out why we feared and dreaded the freak show. The only thing that bothers me is that everyone here is so disgusting-looking.

171

THE HORSE

She noticed with terror that he'd gotten rid of her car.
She could no longer see it through the picture window
where it was always framed, sometimes a bit to the
left or the right, but always there, giving her a real
sense of security. It was a symbol of escape and he
must have sensed that. He always sensed what would
cause her pain. She looked again to make sure the
car hadn't materialized in the second that she hadn't
been looking, but the only thing she could see was
the clean edge of the grass, trimmed neatly, not one
blade growing out onto the small suburban sidewalk,
tidily crew-cut by the high-school kid whom Marvin
accused her of making love with. They hadn't spoken
to each other in a week. Marvin always thought the
sounds the birds made were special code messages of
assignations with her lovers, all the birds in the neighborhood having been enlisted as messengers for that
cause. Not having spoken to Marvin in a week, she
had no idea what he was thinking; she only knew how
much she hated him. She feared speaking and not being
answered. The whole house was adapted to Marvin's
stifled rages. Taciturnity surrounded him like an amni-
onic sac filled with venom, making it possible, merely
by a change in atmosphere, to know whether Marvin
was anywhere in the proximity of herself or the house.

172

She feared that one word from her might cause everything to burst all over, contaminating the Autumn
Warmth Armstrong carpet, and the Drexel One-of-a
Kind furniture with fleur-de-lis furniture covers. She
wandered about the house like a caged animal, caged
by Marvin's feelings about her, her inability to fathom
what he would do next, and how it related to her.
Marvin wasn't ugly at all, but to her every detail about
him was enlarged to the point of hideousness. She'd
notice that one hair of his dark beard had slanted and
grown inward and there was a bit of transparent skin
growing over it, and she'd look at it and look at it
until it assumed gargantuan proportions, and be triumphant over the ugliness of it. If one of his jowls
trembled, she'd feel revulsion. Then triumph.

In the space where her car should have been parked,
a horse rode into view. Marvin was on it. She didn't
know that Marvin could ride. He rode the horse into
the garage and in a few moments came out without it.
I wonder if he got the horse to replace the car, she
thought, but he must know I don't ride. The thought
of it terrified her. She looked up at him as he entered,
as if by his having done something she expected the
heaviness of his anger to have dissipated. Certainly she
expected some sort of explanation for the horse, but
there was none.

She watched him morbidly masticate his dinner, his
lips framed in glowing. grease. He finished the last
spoon of chocolate pudding; he smoothed it over his
tongue in slow motion, while she watched with ab-
sorption and repulsion. When he felt the food drop
onto his tongue he'd close his mouth, not without some
of it dripping out. She was tempted to take the spoon
and wipe it across his lips, collecting the pudding from
one side of his mouth to the other. It was a relief to
have him leave quickly. She sat there in the company
of all the dirty dishes. Actually, his leaving made her

173

angry. Not that he ever did the dishes, but if he sat there while she cleaned up it bothered her less, even though she enjoyed the cleaning more, or didn't have to hate it as much, when he wasn't there.

She began to wonder where he was. She herself never left the house anymore, as he could construe it as suspicious. On the other hand, Marvin was never home anymore. In the morning he'd be out by the time she awoke. Then she'd see him riding the reddish horse past the close houses of the development. Maybe he had a lover. Here she was, locked in the house, and he had a lover. He didn't want her to have one and now he had one. All she did was think about who, where, and when. When she thought the birds were sending messages, she thought, How crazy, I've turned into him.

Isobel never went to see the horse, she never went to touch it. She never went near the garage. It was, she felt, Marvin's very private property, even more so than his underpants, which, though they were exclusively his, she washed, handled, folded, put away—with resentment when she hated him, and proprietarily when she loved him. Even more than his pipes, she had the feeling she shouldn't look at the horse, it was so private it was illicit. One night, late, Marvin wasn't home yet. Isobel was lying in her twin bed with extra-firm Sealy mattress and box spring, with matching Springmaid sheets of Yves St. Laurent design percale, when she heard a faint sound that brought her out of her beginning sleep. It sounded like Marvin having an orgasm. She looked on top of herself for a moment, and he wasn't there, nor was he in his bed. The night was quiet again, except for the scratchy sound of a cricket at sparse intervals. Since there were just high, tiny casement windows in her room, she walked down the carpeted stairs and pulled the large curtains aside slightly at the center of the picture window and looked

174

out. it was an aimless gesture since the sound had seemed to come from the backyard, more force of habit than anything else. Before she got up close to the window she saw a gossamer reflection of herself, transparent, like a ghost, moving gently in her nightgown and peignoir set. She looked lovelier to herself than she'd felt lately, but the fact that she was transparent filled her with terror, since she'd been feeling transparent and now it seemed to have become a reality. She thought that if she didn't do something that involved action immediately, she'd go mad that very instant, so she put on her boots, which were the only shoes she had downstairs, and went outside. She thought of going around the back, but she felt she should keep away from the garage. Her friend Marge, looking out the window that night from across the street, saw Isobel in her nightgown, sitting on an aluminum outdoor chair in the middle of the lawn, staring into space.

Marvin began to sleep out the whole night, from that night on. If he's going to have a lover, she thought, why can't he eat there too, and why can't she do his laundry? Why do I have to cook his dinner, and then be left alone with the dishes? Yet she herself was afraid to break the last contact. One night she was woken by a loud moan. It really sounded like Marvin having an orgasm, but how could that be? It was louder than the last time. Maybe she was going insane and it was haunting her that he had lovers. She should go to a shrink. You should go to a shrink when you hear your husband having orgasms all the time. But she was afraid to go to a shrink, so she tried to think up more logical solutions. For instance, maybe Marvin was next door with her neighbor Rosalie. Certainly their house was close enough to hear a loud orgasm in the deep silence of the night. Maybe that was Rosalie's husband. Maybe all men sound alike. She really didn't know. If it was Marvin with Rosalie, how come he had louder orgasms than with her? She thought of calling up Rosalie and asking her whether that was Marvin at her house having orgasms all the time, so at least she wouldn't think she was going crazy. But Rosalie wouldn't tell her, so it didn't matter. She could say, "Hi, Rosalie. Good morning. How come you sound so refreshed this morning?"

"Well, I just had such a fantastic night's sleep."

"Listen, I've been hearing strange sounds at night; do you?"

"Like what?"

"Just a weird noise."

"I haven't heard anything, but I sleep very heavily."

"Look, Rosalie, was Marvin at your house last night?"

"If he was he sneaked in."

"I thought I heard Marvin having an orgasm in your house last night."

"Don't be silly. Charles was home. You know he'd never stand for Marvin having an orgasm in his house when he was home."

The next day she asked Charles whether he'd been home at around two o'clock in the morning.

He said, "Where else would I be at two o'clock in the morning? I was sleeping because I have to get up and go to work."

"Are you sure?"

"Of course I'm sure, unless my astral body left my physical body and took a journey somewhere, but I try not to because I don't trust Rosalie with my body while I'm gone. She'd nudge me and when I didn't respond she'd pummel me, having no respect for my body. She'd say, 'How come you're always so unresponsive?' and when I didn't respond she'd kick me. Then she'd realize there was something wrong and, not wanting to waste me before I was cold, she'd get on top of me, and gently rape me, and after she'd come and was still lying on top of my soulless, cooling, unbreathing body, she'd cry sleepily, then that same

176

night she'd call the funeral parlor and have me carted out because she hates to keep things around the house (she's exceptionally neat), and the next day, when my soul returned to my body and I opened my eyes, I'd be wearing powder and rouge and lipstick and staring up into the eyes of my mother-in-law and all my other relatives, and all my stuff would be given away, including my car."

Isobel smiled. "Well then, have you been hearing any strange noises?"

"Like what? Wait, I have been hearing a sound like a bull in heat, but I just assumed it was your new horse. Fantastic replacement for the second car. No gas . . . but then it eats hay. And if it gets sick the vet can rip you off just like the garage, unless you get a home-care manual. And those were probably banned by the American Veterinary Association. No, there's no answer for us suburbanites." His voice ripped across the lawn cheerily, then muffled as he entered his car.

Isobel returned to the kitchen, thinking that he wouldn't tell her if he was away or if there was any fooling around, especially in the morning on the front lawn. Maybe Marvin gets into bed with both of them when Charles is asleep, so Charles never knows. But that would be taking an incredible chance, having to keep the bed from moving, and not making any noise, and what about the orgasm? Rosalie and Charles would be in bed, Rosalie waiting for Marvin, Charles fast asleep, slightly pressed against Rosalie. Marvin uses a key and tiptoes into their room, having left his shoes downstairs. He's also stripped off his clothes before entering their bedroom so that he won't make extra noise. Rosalie opens the covers for him on the other side of her. She has to press closer into Charles in order to have enough room for Marvin. Even so, Marvin has almost no room, so he moves on top of Rosalie. His naked body, slightly cool, gives Rosalie goose bumps in her thin brushed-nylon Ohrbach's nightie, but he warms up

177

almost immediately. They kiss without moving the bed; for a second Marvin leans over to look with trepidation at Charles. He's very fearful that Charles will wake, he can't forget Charles for one moment, yet he's excited by the fact that Charles is there and might wake up, like making love without any birth control when you know you're ovulating. It's fun to make love without moving, like a challenge, superexciting. Rosalie doesn't move at all, or slightly, slowly, around, and Marvin, on top, has a bit more leverage if he doesn't move the mattress or the blanket covering the three of them. As he holds Rosalie, his arm is against Charles, who feels warm, as he slowly and subtly moves his whole organ into Rosalie and out, each of them enjoying the enforced resistance against becoming frenetic. Rosalie chokes back noises; they stop and look at Charles, who is still sleeping. Rosalie's more careful and buries her head into the pillow. They both come in a suspended tension of the body, externally still, slightly raised off the mattress. Then Marvin bellows. As soon as he hears himself he becomes silent and they both suspend breathing, not even daring to look over at Charles. After what seems to be an enormous lapse of time, Marvin, without looking around, slides off Rosalie, kisses her goodbye as she pulls down her uncomfortable nonabsorbent nylon nightie, and crawls out of the room, dragging his clothes with him to the stairs like a retriever.

Marvin rode up to the door on the horse and sat down for his silent breakfast. Isobel was tempted to burn the toast to see whether that would get him to say something—for instance, "The toast is burnt"—but maybe he'd do something violent, silently, like look at the toast, walk over to her, put his thick, square-fingered, reddish hands around her neck, and begin to press passionately—but with a restraint similar to that which he used on Rosalie and which would save her life. After Marvin finished he wiped some egg and crumbs

178

off his mouth, crumpled the napkin next to his dish, and, outside, lifted himself onto the horse. Isobel watched him mount the horse. Even while she hated him, his getting on the horse had a sensual quality that made her very jealous of him and his life. She almost desired him again. For an instant it was like being in love with him again. Certainly it was a new Marvin, not the same slovenly movement of slipping heavily down into the low front seat of the car. Then she realized that now he was riding the horse to work.

Maybe he's hiding his music students in the basement and making love with them there while I'm asleep, thought Isobel. She pictured herself descending the cold stairs to the basement in the dark of night. It was mostly dark and very cold, but a slight light shone from the laundry room, lighting her way. She knew she never left a light on in the laundry room. She padded quietly in, her feet totally noiseless on concrete. It felt cold and scrapy, like pumice, as she approached the room from the side so that she could just peek around the corner of the doorway. She almost tripped on the music stands, then adjusted her eyes and made sure she saw all their metallic lines. Terrified to get her head far enough into the doorway in order to be able to see something, finally she did, and saw that no one was looking at her. The light from the bare bulb in the ceiling hurt her eyes and threw a cold, harsh light over the whole laundry room with its cold white Sears Kenmore washer and dryer, and white meat-club freezer. Marvin and his music student were lying on the damp concrete floor on some towels they'd removed from the dryer and thrown down. She was angry that they were using her clean towels. Is that what she washed towels for? The girl was lying on her blue-and-olive Picasso-print velvet-pile towel with her sweater on and her skirt pulled up around her waist. Her nylon stockings lay beside her, limp and deflated like a pair of oversized used condoms. Marvin

179

was lying next to her, with his shirt on and his pants down around his thighs. His skin looked incredibly white in the harsh light, in between the dark shirt and pants, and showing through his dark body hair. He appeared more naked than he'd ever been, even though he was wearing clothes. The girl was moaning because Marvin had his hand up her vagina and every time he jiggled his fingers there was a sucking sound, as if the washing machine was going on WASH. She had her hand around his penis, which was limp and yellow, its head peering over her clenched hand like a newborn kitten. Perspiration poured down Marvin's body and onto her towel as his body clenched with the effort of obtaining an erection. The girl, moaning louder now, looked down at her hand and opened it, watched the tiny thing drop to one side, and murmured in a frenzy of passion and frustration, "Marvin marvin marvin marvin . . ." Marvin removed his hand from her vagina, looked around for a second, and picked up her alto recorder from the floor where it lay beside her music book and shoes. He looked at it for a moment, as though trying to decide which end would be best, and moved it gently toward her as if it were an extension of himself. She lifted her head, leaned on one elbow, and grabbed his wrist. "No, no, Marvin, Marvin, no." She held his wrist in a deadlock for a moment, then pulled his hand toward her, lay down again, and Marvin masterfully inserted the recorder, mouthpiece first, into her vagina. By that time Marvin had an erection, but the woman was coming so Marvin considerately rammed her with the recorder while she writhed and panted. Then, the recorder still sticking out of her vagina, Marvin put his whole body over hers, but way above, held up by his hands, with elbows stiff, and on his toes. She put her hand around his cock once again, and moved it up and down like a piston, never releasing her hold. Marvin became stiffer and stiffer. Over her, he looked like the Verrazano Bridge. He gave two grunts, then his great bellow, as his sperm

180

shot first way up between her breasts and then on her abdomen, falling on her doubleknit sweater and suede skirt, respectively. All of a sudden the bridge collapsed. His hand over her fell into the sperm. He looked into her eyes for a moment and said, "I'm sorry. . . . Lucky this is the laundry. You can wash them."

Marge came over. "I thought I saw you out on the lawn the other morning at about 3 A.M."

"Maybe it was me. I'm going crazy, Marge, I think I hear Marvin coming all the time. It even wakes me up from sleep. I didn't want to tell anyone, because Marvin doesn't sleep here anymore and I don't know where he is, but I must be haunted by it because I hear him having orgasms all the time, and I don't know where the sound is coming from."

Marge said, "Maybe it's the horse. You know, there's not much difference between the sound of a man and the sound of a horse neighing." Isobel offered Marge a piece of cake. "No, thanks, I'm not eating Entenmann's cake today. I ate fourteen in the past three days, so I'm trying to fast today. There's a new swami who comes to the house and gives private yoga lessons. Everyone's been using him, but I have to clean out my system first. It would be a waste of money to have that swami come and do yoga with fourteen Entenmann's cakes floating around my body."

Isobel made up her mind to check out the horse. She got out of bed at about three that night, not knowing why she went to bed at all, except that that's what she always did at night. She put on Marvin's bathrobe because she felt suddenly chilled in a deep way that pervaded her entire body internally through all her organs and left her hands glowing white and her lips tight and blanched, and a pair of green fur slippers Marvin had given her one Christmas, and went out through the side door and slowly up the driveway, toward the garage, trying not to crunch the gravel, which

181

was damp with the night air. It was not a clear night, it was foggy. There was a nimbus of moisture around everything, with a faint rainbow aura. Strings of hay scattered all about reflected the moonlight. Funny she never noticed it before. A slight odor of horse and hay emanated moistly from the closed garage. She was panicky as she bent down for the garage door handle, not knowing how quiet she could be, how quiet she had to be. It depended on what was going on in there. For instance, when she opened it, Marvin could be just sitting there, watching her open it. As she gently lifted the door a few inches—and it made hardly any noise (it must have been oiled recently)— a faint light, reddish, exuded through the crack, shining garishly on the grass. She waited a moment and pulled the door higher. Fearful and impatient, she tried to peer under it without raising it more, but without success. She just got an incredible whiff of barn smell that was staggering. Pausing another moment in the silence she could hear a very gentle breathing that calmed her because it was not the breathing of someone who was waiting for the door to open but the breathing of someone who was sleeping. She took a chance and raised it more. The reddish glow from the light assailed her, along with the smell, before any visual image assimilated. Then she saw that the glow came from a red bulb in a rough socket in the unfinished garage interior. There was hay all over, cobwebs, bags of feed, a pile of horseshit, and, in the corner, on a large pile of hay and some filthy quilted horse blankets, lay Marvin, naked, partially covered with purplish-gray and greenish-purple blankets, the exposed portions of his body pink and red in the glowing light. The horse was lying against him, nearly cradling him, one heavy foreleg over Marvin's body, hair reddish brown, semiretracted penis gently resting against Marvin's leg, gleaming whitely, as it was shielded from the light by his own upper thigh. Isobel's first thought was that she didn't know horses lay down when they slept. She

182

stepped back out of the garage and just looked at the scene without thinking, just let it sit there, an image. Then it occurred to her what a ludicrous scene was displayed to the people who lived across the street, if they happened to be up, gazing through their picture window; scrupulously and silently she closed the garage door and padded back to bed.

She looked at Marvin with new eyes, as if she didn't know him. He became more interesting to her and even strangely sexually attractive. At the same time, she felt power over him, having seen him—without him seeing her—revealed in an unguarded moment of truth. When he ate his meals in silence she could almost laugh at his pretense of dignity. She was losing her fear of him, yet she was in awe of him for expanding into other realms of living without her. Suddenly life, which was such a drag, became very exciting. She couldn't wait to spy some more on Marvin and the horse. She had to figure out some way to observe Marvin when he was awake to see what exactly he did, but that seemed pretty impossible. She couldn't very well open the garage door while Marvin was awake. She could hide somewhere before he came in, but even if Marvin didn't sense her presence, the horse would. She could go in and meet the horse now to get him used to her. She considered asking Marge's advice, but didn't want to tell her yet. She walked to the garage feeling the same fear she felt when she got her first air conditioner, and she had to relate to it herself, without anyone else to adjust it for her. She decided to call on the horse first, but if Marvin rode the horse to work, how could she? She thought that at least she'd go into the garage and leave her smell around during the afternoon, and sometime right after dinner she'd hide in the garage till Marvin finally came in for the night. As she walked to the garage this time, her high heels crunched in the gravel and her ankle twisted. She felt a strange excitement and a sensation of doing something wrong. Even though she wasn't doing anything actually wrong, she was fearful of being discovered. But Marvin was at work and so was the horse. She realized that she thought of the garage not as Marvin's but as the domain of the horse. Marvin was a guest, just as she was. The garage smelled like a horse—it was furnished with horse stuff right down to the horseshit in the corner. The hay tickled her ankles. It had a rich smell that was almost unbearable. She lay down on it to test it out and it prickled, so she put one of the funky blankets under her. When next she opened her eyes it took her a moment to orient herself, then she realized that she'd fallen asleep in the garage. Having slept there, she was more at peace there, more like she belonged. With the door closed, she felt she could die of the fumes—but at least they weren't carbon monoxide. She wanted to go back to the house and recover for a while, but she had no idea what time it was and resolved not to miss her chance tonight. Chance at what she wasn't sure. There was a flavor of evening in the air even though the garage had no windows. She piled some hay behind two monster bags of feed and covered most of herself with a blanket. She couldn't understand why it didn't bother her to lie in all the junk and get her clothes dirty. She felt a great sense of abandon. Suddenly the garage door opened with a giant proprietary swing on its runners and the whole door was up. There was a rush of cool air. Isobel felt exposed, but apparently no one suspected that she was there. Almost immediately Marvin slammed the door shut behind him and came over to a feed bag. He seemed to be removing some of the stuff—perhaps it was oats—but she didn't see what he was doing because she wanted to remain hidden. She was more titillated and stimulated than nervous.

When next she had the courage to look up, Marvin and the horse were picnicking. The horse was eating

184

oats or something out of her kelly-green Melmac garbage pail, and Marvin had three bags from MacDonald's sitting next to him and all his food spread out: a Big Mac cheeseburger, two packages of french fries, a Coke, and coffee. She felt a surge of anger that Marvin didn't even miss her the first time she wasn't in the house to make his dinner. He wasn't cursing or anything, he just bought his own whatever he liked. Certainly she wouldn't serve him that. The realization that she was getting out of preparing a meal didn't assuage her anger. He seemed to prefer eating with the horse also. He almost looked happy. She watched every motion carefully. She watched him squeeze his ketchup out of those soft plastic containers, which he opened with his teeth then manipulated from the bottom up until every drop of ketchup was spread on the cheeseburger. Then he opened five more and methodically poured them out all over the two packs of french fries. He's really going to the dogs, she thought. He had ketchup on the corners of his mouth. He wolfed everything down and reclined on a bunch of junk. The horse ate slowly. She watched his mouth move, fascinated. She'd never watched a horse so closely before. The only horse she'd ever seen was in *National Velvet*. She realized that she never really looked at the horses even when she saw other horse movies. The horse seemed to gather up a mouthful of the oats by gently manipulating them into his mouth, using only his soft lips, then raising his head slowly, as if swallowing a pill, he allowed the oats to slip beyond his enormous front teeth, which he exposed for a moment between each bite. Then he chewed carefully, his jaw moving slowly from side to side, and back again, once in every few chews tossing his head like a woman throwing long hair out of her face with a shrug. After a while the horse sniffed around, his nostrils opening and closing like a jellyfish propelling itself along the Caribbean Sea. He sniffed the McDonald's bags, the leftover french fries, and began chewing them up. He masticated all the remains, including the bags and cardboard hotcup. He even gets the horse to clean up after him. Men really have it made, thought Isobel. Then the horse hovered over Marvin himself, looked into his eyes, shot out his tongue, and gently licked the ketchup from the corners of his mouth, and remained there for a moment, hovering over Marvin lovingly. Marvin seemed to be aroused by the horse's hot breath and began to respond. He gazed lovingly into the horse's eyes. Isobel was embarrassed at witnessing that exchange. They both began to breathe heavily, like the grating of onions on the fine side of a grater. Marvin got up and, delicately removing his gaze from the magnetic stare of the horse, swiftly undressed. He lay his clothing over the grain sack that Isobel was hiding behind. She saw them hung over her side, piece by piece. A tiny bit of Marvin smell emanated from them, if she could smell anything over the stable smell, but she seemed to be adjusting, as she almost didn't smell that anymore. Now that Marvin was totally naked, she had no idea what he was going to do, but all he did was lie down again, almost exactly where he'd been reclining when the horse licked his lips. Wasn't he going to do anything? It was becoming damp and chilly in this garage. Marvin's penis lay across his thigh like a cucumber in a bed of chicory. She was shivering, but Marvin, naked, didn't appear to be cold at all. The horse moved closer to him again. For a moment the horse's head, glowing redly, obliterated Marvin's face from view, so she watched his penis, which slowly tumesced. It began to fill out all the loose skin very leisurely, at one point it jerked upward a bit on his thigh; then it got larger still, until it stood straight up, almost black in the red light, and pointed navelward. Marvin gently patted the horse's head, and turned it at the same time, in the gentlest way, so that the horse saw Marvin's enormous erection. Isobel saw the horse inhale deeply, his nostrils flaring sensuously as he stood there and looked. Then he looked at Marvin for a

186

moment and slowly unfurled his tongue, like a flag rolling out on a windless day, bits of saliva dripping from the sides of his mouth. Marvin lay there totally passive, melting into the sacks under him, practically two-dimensional, while the horse gently snuffled his nose against Marvin's penis, and a drop of horse saliva fell on the underside and slowly dripped down until it was trapped in his pubic hair like a bit of semen. With utmost delicacy, the horse, beginning at Marvin's pubic hair, lay his thin, flat tongue against his penis and licked upward, the flatness of his tongue practically surrounding the whole cock like a pig in a blanket. Marvin closed his eyes as if in pain, sucked in his breath, and raised his hips in immediate ecstasy. Then suddenly Isobel became cognizant of the horse's penis, swelling between his red legs, white and veiny, enormous as a club. She experienced a strange, momentary, ripping jealousy that Marvin himself should have found the most likely lover. The horse continued his sensuous licking of Marvin's organ, saliva spraying all over, Marvin moaning and writhing around, his eyeballs rolled up into his head. Isobel was becoming extremely excited. She' didn't know who she desired, Marvin or the horse. She was becoming breathlessly appetitive watching the movements of the gradual soothing tongue, incredibly wrapping and licking and moistening Marvin's fat purple penis, and she touched her own vagina. With great difficulty she pulled down her underpants, trying to maintain silence, and felt the dirty blanket and some stray straw under her behind. Just as she touched her clitoris, some saliva spray from the horse dropped on it, feeling cool for a moment. That drop of liquid from the horse's mouth drove her wild in itself, but when she moved her hand it lubricated her and she came immediately, frenetically silent. She had the feeling that the horse was aware of her presence and of the sexual thing between them too. She suddenly felt compelled to pull up her pants and rearrange her skirt. She was able to observe more objectively now.

187

The horse stopped for a moment, licked Marvin's balls, then the insides of his thighs and then ran his flat tongue all over Marvin's straining body like a vacuum cleaner; there wasn't a part he missed. Then he gently nudged Marvin at the small of his back, where Marvin's skin was soft, smooth, and white, and at that ever-so-slight touch, Marvin turned over onto his abdomen. The horse licked his slightly hairy ass, the center of his tongue entering the crack slightly. Marvin's back began to arch more and more, until the horse stood over him and gently nudged Marvin's ass with the thick head of his own white penis, and at the touch Marvin let out a soulful moan. Then the horse moved over Marvin until Marvin was completely cradled between and beneath the horse's legs, as if in a house. Breathing heavily, Marvin rubbed his back and head in a very loving way along the horse's chest and under-belly, which were right above him; and then, now and again balancing his body on his two knees and one arm, he caressed a foreleg, running his hand stretched out, as if to achieve the maximum sensual area, along the whole flank and down the leg, from outside in and inside out, in a very loving way. Then, bracing himself for the pressure from the horse, Marvin, arms trembling as they held up his weight, hands making marks in the crusty dirt of the floor, nearly fell forward, but remained up on his hands and knees, and a silent scream was emitted from his wide-open mouth and bugged-out eyes, a look of pain and pleasure both, as Isobel saw that somehow the horse had inserted part of his penis. Incredibly gentle, the horse didn't thrust powerfully but, in order not to hurt Marvin, just moved so tenderly around and around, never forcing. Marvin was still on his trembling arms, moving his behind gently around and emitting moans and cries incessantly, his own organ, swelled to an incomparable size for it, was there in front of him, and Isobel thought for a moment, What a waste. She pictured a smaller animal under Marvin, and in fact it could go on like that forever, until

at the bottom a dragonfly was making it with a roach.
She watched as if hypnotized, his penis moving closer
and closer to the floor with every movement, until it
finally touched one of the sacks, and at that instant,
as if it were a signal, Marvin and the horse both
neighed loudly and came together, Marvin's sperm
spurting out and some of it hitting his chest, where
it hung in the hair for a moment as the reddish light
lent the milky drops a pinkish halo. Suddenly Marvin
dropped off his arms and lay, exhausted, where he
fell, on top of his own sperm. Isobel got up to leave
the moment Marvin fell asleep, and she didn't have to
wait long. Lying exactly as he'd fallen, he remained
and began snoring. The horse lay down next to him
without moving away, so Marvin lay cradled between
the horse's limbs. For some reason, Isobel no longer
feared that the horse would give away her presence. As
she walked on tiptoe to the garage door, she looked
at the horse and saw his deep, expressionless gaze
follow her until she was outside the garage. The last
thing she saw as she quietly pulled down the garage
door was the horse's one large, dark eye that was still
visible over Marvin's slumped body, looking at her,
a sharp dot of reflected light emanating from it. As
she continued to close the door the dot of light disappeared, but the eye remained steady. When the door
shut completely, shocked with the sweet smell of the
air, she found herself alone in the dark, moist evening.

Marvin stopped riding the horse to work. Isobel wondered why and suspected that he'd seen her in the
garage that night. She feared that he was planning some
sort of plot to discover her in his domain, with his
horse, which in itself shouldn't seem suspect, but in
view of her own desires, it was, since she thought day
and night of that scene, and of herself taking Marvin's
place. After the morning she saw Marvin leave for
work without the horse, she didn't dare go near the

189

garage. Feeling very uneasy, she decided to call Marge and tell her about the horse.

"Hello, Marge, how's your yoga?"

"Just beautiful, I'm finding my center."

"Where is it?"

"I can't describe it. Why don't you come over for some banana bread?" asked Marge. "I bake my own bread now, and only with organic ingredients."

"Okay, but don't you have your lesson today with the swami?"

"I can't take it today because my system is full. I already ate six banana breads today."

Marge's house smelled sweet and delicious from baking. Marge herself was wearing a transparent Indian shirt which exposed the outlines of her girdle, rolled down at the waist, where, at its boundaries, it absolutely lost the power to contain the waves of flesh that rolled over it. Her legs stuck out from under the shirt like two white, sticky loaves of unbaked bread left to rise under a moist towel, and made a comforting, rhythmic flapping sound as Marge walked about the kitchen, preparing Mu tea (from sixteen herbs) and slicing banana bread for Isobel.

"It's too moist. I like it moist, but this is too moist, don't you think?"

"No, it's just perfect, I love it moist. It's more like a dessert than bread, but I like it."

"It's like banana-bread pudding," laughed Marge as she delicately dropped a tiny tablet of saccharin into her Mu tea from a tiny silver spoon. Isobel watched it bubble ominously until it disappeared and then she was confronted by Marge's enormous nipple, which rested on the edge of the table and was clearly visible through her shirt.

"I think I've fallen in love with the swami," Marge confided. "And I think he loves me too, he just believes in patience. I told Fred and he says I have his blessings as long as I continue to cook meat for him."

"Now what makes you think the swami loves you?" asked Isobel, sinking into the soporific sauna-bath sensation of Marge's kitchen and their conversation.

"Because he said to me, and he looked strangely and deeply into my eyes as he said it, and his eyes emanated love . . .

'Serve thou the true guru, lovingly and with
    single-minded devotion;
Know that the true guru is the holy of holies,
Who fulfills all the desires of thy mind.
Thou gatherest the blessing, the fruits thy
    heart longs for.'

"That means that if I love him he'll fulfill all the desires I have in my mind."

. "I think it means all the desires *of* thy mind . . . not of the body," said Isobel; then she recalled the enormous, dark, expressionless eye of the horse, and felt sudden fear and desire.

"Listen, Marge, I think I'm in love also."

. "With who? Marvin?"

"No, no, with the horse."

"With the horse." Marge just repeated the last words.

"I'm not sure what love is, Marge, whether I just desire him sexually or whether that's what falling in love is, because I don't know him, but I can see that he's the most loving per—. . . animal I've ever seen, and I really desire him. I think about him all the time. I'm going mad. But I think he likes me too."

- "Well, go ahead, do what you like. It's never wrong to love. This is interesting. Maybe the horse is between incarnations. He'll probably be human in his next life. But you probably won't, so if not now you may never get together."

"I know," Isobel said, "but I'm afraid Marvin suspects. He's not like Fred. He's very possessive and capable of violence. I'm not sure if he'd be possessive

191

of me or of the horse, but I'm scared. He doesn't take the horse to work anymore and I'm afraid it's a trap."

"Oh, no, Fred told me that they just don't like the horse waiting outside the Curran Building in Hempstead all day, and the owners of the building asked him to leave the horse home."

With that explanation, Isobel felt a sudden surge of joy and relief. She went home to visit the horse.

This time when she opened the door to the garage it was with a fear of relating to the horse, not so much the fear of being discovered. She was fearful of being rejected. She opened the door swiftly—after all, it was her garage too. Who had worked to finish putting Marvin through music school . . . and then law school? She was wearing something that exposed her midriff and her navel, which she felt was the most sensuous part of her body, and she had rubbed some musk body oil into it, and rubbed it into her hair. The garage still stank, but the stench had sexual implications to Isobel by this time. One quality the horse possessed that Isobel loved, as she saw him turn his head and look at her without surprise, was his acceptance of everything. He had such a totally open expression. She felt she could be perfectly free with him, be herself for once. There was nothing he expected of her, or an image he seemed to have of her which he projected, and that she had to fulfill or else risk his love being withdrawn. She had the feeling that with this horse she could be as passionate as she liked or do anything she liked, without turning him off. She rolled the garage door down behind her and turned to face the horse, who was standing there looking bored, nudging a pile of hay but not eating. He looked directly into her eyes and she felt as if she were floating and her whole body was being absorbed into his through those orbs, and when his nostrils twitched she felt a mad feeling of love and desire. She realized that it was the angle at which his nose swept down from his brow, and the

192

way it flared out a bit at the bottom, that was so incredibly sensual to her, almost as if that simple aesthetic combination could, like magic, be the whole cause of this passion. She stood there for a moment before walking over to him. With great joy, she saw that he was walking over to her first, and she was pleased that he was making some kind of move. The fact that he was was like all her fantasies of the past days come true. As if aware of her attempts to be seductive, the horse sniffed her navel with his moist, quivering nostrils. Isobel was too happy to feel anything more than just elation at being there with the horse. She looked more closely at him, touched his face gently, snuffled his mane with her nose. When he lifted one thin black lip for one moment, she noticed that his large front teeth weren't even, one stuck out in front of the other. As she was having dental work done, and had temporary jackets on, one of her front teeth stuck out in front of the other too. She whispered goodbye to the horse. It seemed extremely symbolic that they had similar teeth. As she walked down the driveway she wondered why, after all those sexual fantasies, she didn't actually feel like having sex with the horse when she was with him. She recalled what Marvin had said when she first met him: "I like to get to know someone before I go to bed with them. Do you?" And the horse didn't press her either. She was glad he felt the same way.

The next day, when Marvin went into the garage before he left for work, Isobel felt an unexpected twinge of jealousy, since he'd already spent the night in there. As soon as he was gone, she rummaged around for some kind of offering or gift she and the horse could enjoy together. For a moment she couldn't think what horses liked besides sugar, which was no good for his teeth and which she wouldn't be able to partake of with him, then decided on two magnificent reddish-black apples. This was the first time in a long while that she felt really excited to be alive. She experienced a strong

193

sense of release and abandon. She went out in her nightgown, barefoot, an apple in each hand, like Eve. She thought, as she opened the garage door, that maybe she should clean it up a bit, tidy it, and get rid of that odor, and then she realized that she didn't want that kind of relationship again. She wasn't willing to have her ability to clean be one of her desirable traits. If he didn't like her this way, too bad. The horse looked up when she entered, but he never looked surprised. That was one of the qualities she found fascinating about him. She held the apple out to him and he nudged it for a moment with his soft mouth closed, then he raised one of his lips in a weird way and Isobel saw his crooked tooth. For one horrible moment she thought, What am I doing here with this ugly creature? but in a second that passed. The horse took one bite of the apple, which nearly obliterated it, core and all, except for a tiny piece left sitting in her hand which revealed a glaring whiteness in contrast to the almost-black skin, and two tiny capillaries of maroon. In surprise, she handed over the second apple, which at first he only sniffed, as he was still chewing the other, with sideways motions of his head and some slobbering. She watched him with wonder, realizing how well she knew Marvin and how strange this was. The horse stopped chewing for a moment, looked into Isobel's eyes, wrapped his mouth around her whole apple, and remained that way, with his soft lips touching her palm. For the first time since she'd watched Marvin and the horse, she felt sexually excited. As the horse finished her apple too, she said, "You pig!" and laughed. Marvin was a slob, and a hog too, but this horse was even worse. Somehow, she felt all her standards for men or lovers drop away. She felt flexible, able to accept, to find out, free. It doesn't matter, she told herself, I can afford this relationship now. She touched the horse all over his soft face with its coating of short fur, like suede, ran her fingers across his eyelids, causing him to close his eyes and flare his nostrils in that way that appealed

194

to her so much. She put her nose against his and felt his warm breath surround her face like a General Electric facial sauna, and an enormous feeling of desire and abandon overcame her. She began kissing the horse wildly, all over his gentle furred protuberances and concavities, all new to her, grabbed his soft, silky mane, and, clutching the light brown hair tightly, buried her fists in it, while the horse, his nose becoming hot, nuzzled her all over. She collapsed where she'd been standing, not caring whether it was clean or not, and closed her eyes. For an instant she reminded herself of Marvin. The horse took her nightgown between his teeth and lifted it. He pressed his lips gently all over her sentient body, just a soft pressure with gentle furred edges that drove her wild. He pressed, gently pressed, into her pubic hair and along the insides of her thighs, which she spread for him in abandon. She could never picture doing this with Marvin—though she'd felt like it once in a while—as Marvin would think she was lewd. She had the feeling that it would frighten Marvin. The horse continued his gentle pressure all over her body, and again and again she felt his hot nose and lips press her pubic hair and her hidden clitoris. She raised her hips off the garage floor, and felt the horse's large, flat tongue, with a firm muscular pressure, press in between her labia, felt its wet heat encompass her clitoris for a moment before sliding down its length, giving her the most voluptuous sensation she'd ever imagined, and press slightly into the opening of her vagina, and return slowly upward again. She had a desire to move her hips but, wanting to prolong everything, and enjoying the horse, who needed no assistance in pleasing her, she allowed—even consciously trying to remain still—the horse to repeat his slow, endless licks from one end of her labial opening to the other, penetrating subtly, increasingly deeper into her vagina each time he passed it. And she, allowing the waves of sensation, which she felt all over her body and deeply into her thighs, to sweep over her until they became

195

greater and greater, too much to bear—no, she couldn't bear them, she began to moan, but the horse retained his slowness, and she began to grunt and shout, "No, no, no, no, no," as she felt her body contract endlessly. The walls of her vagina clenched tightly around the horse's whole trembling tongue, she felt her eyes roll into their sockets, and then she relaxed. The horse began nudging her on the side. For an instant she felt annoyance and no desire to do anything more, until she saw the horse's penis floating toward her, bobbing up and down lightly, as in water. Defying gravity, it hung there, not down but almost parallel with the horse's underbelly, its thick tip practically staring her in the eye. She allowed the horse to push her limp body over as he might one of the empty sacks, and she lay there on her stomach, her nightgown across her neck and through one armhole like a banner worn in a Miss America pageant. She lay there for a moment and found herself not relating to him at all. She was lying on some coarse muslin sack and gently brushed her fingers along one spot as she often did while falling asleep, feeling the soft brush of the fabric with the very tips of her fingers. She looked up for a moment and saw, glowing like a pink fluorescent light bulb, the horse's cock. Then she felt it move under her from behind, until it rubbed her clitoris, as the tip pushed all the way in front, touching her belly. She became excited again, but was slightly terrified by the size of the horse's organ, which she hadn't realized was that enormous. She had an urge to run, then thought it wouldn't be fair to run off without satisfying the horse. She raised herself onto her hands and knees, as she'd seen Marvin do, and she could see, by looking down under herself, the horse's bulbous organ, now appearing dark against her own white skin, lying under her, almost reaching to her breasts. Then she watched it moving away slowly, like being in the last car of a train and watching through the tunnel as the train begins to move, and she felt its whole length move back along her vaginal opening.

196

The horse repeated this movement a few times and Isobel watched from underneath as the penis came toward her and retreated, until she had to close her eyes and strain her whole body back. She no longer cared how large his penis was, she could absorb it. She pushed back more and more, and felt him insert the tip, just the tip, gently into her vagina, where it remained still, stretching her tightly, and feeling heavy, an incredible weight, like a pressurized balloon. She pressed back more, until her whole vagina felt filled—no, her whole body, like a turkey ready for the oven. The horse never tried to insert the full length of his cock. He allowed her to move softly, however she wished, until she came again, and still the horse hadn't had an orgasm. Then he began moving harder, harder and harder, being gentle but still hurting somewhat, a hurt that she knew she was enjoying, as she cried and cried with pain and pleasure, and the horse neighed as he came. Then she realized that she'd forgotten her diaphragm. She wondered whether horse sperm fertilized human eggs. Could she give birth to a centaur? Even the horse's detumescent penis fitted her so tightly it made a small pop as he removed it, like the swollen cork in vintage wine. She caressed his underbelly lovingly, amazed at the incredible consideration and gentleness he'd shown restraining the major portion of his strength not to hurt her. She lay for a moment inside the C shape that he made when lying on his side with his four legs straight out, protected as if in a cave, a warm cave, and she had no idea how much time had passed. She began to feel panicky. She arose, feeling dirty and scrubby for the first time, and brushed herself off. She felt she should say something to the horse since they'd just made love and she didn't want him to think she wanted him only for sex. She looked at the horse, wondering whether he expected anything, and it appeared as if he didn't. He still had his blank, open expression, but warmer, tired, lids hanging lower, relaxed, slicing his eye in half. She noticed some grit in

197

the corner of each eye and, for want of any other expression of tenderness, picked it out with great pleasure,
and scraped the little bit of dried moisture that looked
like an old tear from underneath the grit, stroked his
silky nose, and departed. Her neighbors saw her running down the driveway in her nightgown, hopping
gingerly through the gravel, in midafternoon.

Rosalie stopped her as she opened the screen door.
"What are you doing in your nightgown at this time
of day? You sure have a leisurely life."

"Oh, I was just cleaning out the garage for the
horse," said Isobel, blushing. "I began in the morning
and got so involved I hadn't realized what time it was."
It was true that now, outside the barn, her life had
the aspect of a dream. She couldn't get everything
connected, and felt strangely discombobulated. Standing there talking with Rosalie, she felt all the horse's
seminal fluid running thickly down one leg, past the
bottom of her white permanent-press cotton batiste
nightgown, then, as if once begun it couldn't be con-
tained, it began running down the other leg too, tickling
annoyingly. Isobel said, "I think I left the oven on,"
and ran inside. Rosalie watched Isobel close the door
behind her, the back of her hair and nightgown covered with straw.

Isobel realized that the horse was the best lover she'd
ever had. Yet her life and his were so different, he
could never become part of hers. She couldn't think
how to integrate this affair with the rest of her life.
She wondered whether the horse liked her. She'd been
so passive, but she really'd felt free to enjoy herself
for the first time.

"How is it?" asked Marge.

"He's the best lover I've ever had! It's just incredible."

"Really?"

"Yes. Why don't you try it, Marge?"

"No, thanks. I can't see it," said Marge.

Isobel pictured Marge with the horse. She'd waddle up the driveway, with her shopping cart, full of provisions, bobbing along the gravel behind her. She'd roll up the door, push the cart in, then enter herself. "I wish you had a refrigerator here," she says to the horse. "I don't want these cream puffs to get spoiled." The horse watches as she bustles about, removing groceries from the cart and setting up a picnic on his favorite blanket. Then she relaxes in between the pastries and a dish with ham, capicola, headcheese, and bologna. "Whew," she says as she begins to slice some Jewish rye. Still the horse watches silently. "Have a sandwich," says Marge. "What would you like on it?" She holds up the dish so that the horse can see the choices, and she looks on amazed as he gobbles everything on the dish in one minute, leaving just a morsel of something unrecognizable that goes flying off into a corner.

"It's so nice to cook for someone who enjoys food," she says, ceasing her now-useless bread slicing and proceeding to eat some cake. She picks up a cannoli delicately with two fingers, transferring it to her other hand, where she holds it from underneath and moves it toward her mouth that way, as if it were a loving offering, only she puts it in too far, in her hurry to eat it before the horse does. In her effort to chew too much at one time, some thick cannoli cream creeps out along her lips, which the horse, who is standing over her, immediately licks off. Marge is immobile for an instant while she seems to be deciding whether she wants to continue eating or look into the feeling she got when the horse licked her lips, and then she gets up and removes her clothing, heavily and methodically, including her girdle. She starts by rolling it down over itself at the waist and then continues to roll until, when she takes it off, it's like a thick rubber band, which she throws on top of her other clothes with the agility of a cowboy with a lariat. She lies down right on top of all the food, wriggles in comfortably, and begins emptying éclairs and cannoli on herself, rubbing the cream all over. The horse obligingly begins to lick it off. "Ohhhhhhhh," says Marge. "You smell so male. Like avocádo. With garlic. Ohh, that feels good!" She continues frosting herself with various types of creams, marbleizing her body in egg cream, whipped cream, and cream cheese, plastering it expertly into her pubic hair, moaning as the horse licks it off. Then she notices his erection. "My god," she says, "it's as big as a banana bread!" To protect herself she begins stuffing cannoli, cherries, and nuts into her vagina until it looks like the horn of plenty. Gathering up her courage, she takes the horse's penis in·her hand and rubs cream all over that. She licks it off in a flurry of activity, while the horse attempts to eat all the goodies out of her vagina.

"Wouldn't you be jealous if I made love with your horse?" asked Marge.

"You don't understand," said Isobel. "Because I love him it doesn't mean that he's mine. We're having a very successful nonexclusive relationship. You forget that Marvin is also the horse's lover." Then she asked, "Whatever happened with the swami?" as she realized that Marge was eating a bologna sandwich.

"He's afraid. Afraid of me, and of strong feelings. Finally, I couldn't stand it any longer and I tried to seduce him, and he absolutely refused to be seduced. He doesn't know what love means or how to give it or receive it, and yet he talks about it all the time. How can he teach it if he's incapable of it? Since he rejected me I've gained fifteen pounds," she pouted.

"Love isn't only sexuality," said Isobel.

"Yes, but if you do love, how can you deny someone that last expression, the most intimate? That's running. And that's what he did—he ran. So fast."

Isobel smiled as she pictured the swami, gnarled and robed, running down Maple Lane, and felt glad to be spared analyzing about love. She felt a sense of superiority about her relationship with the horse.

One morning when she went to the garage she found the horse lying listlessly. His ears didn't even retract slightly as they did when he was exhausted but wanted to acknowledge her presence. His eyes showed no life whatsoever; they seemed to be turned inside out. For a moment she thought he was dead, but his body was rising and falling rhythmically as he breathed. She was in a panic . . . afraid that Marvin would blame her if anything happened to his horse. She listened for a rasping in his breathing, as the only horse illness she had heard of was pneumonia. Had Marvin ridden him in the rain? She felt his head, which was moist with perspiration but not at all feverish, and patted him. She kissed him all over his face. He squinted when she kissed him, as if he had a fly on his face, but he didn't respond to her. Then he closed his eyes and, in exasperation, she left. She was terrified. She couldn't imagine what was wrong and she couldn't do anything until Marvin came home and discovered it himself. And what if there was nothing wrong with the horse, but he was just rejecting her? After all, he also had Marvin, and she never felt too secure with non-exclusive relationships. All along she'd imagined that she had a complicity with the horse that excluded Marvin, and somehow she felt that the horse preferred her to Marvin, as she preferred the horse to Marvin. Yet now she faced the possibility that perhaps his relationship with Marvin had reached an intensity that was going to exclude her. She walked around the house drinking wine and weeping, not daring to even check on the horse. She wept as if the horse had left her forever, though she reminded herself from time to time that that wasn't the reality, only a small possibility. By the time Marvin came home, she was nauseated with fear and sorrow. As soon as she heard the garage door roll up, she ran to the mirror to try to pull herself together. She looked like a dried apricot. She quickly obliterated any sign of emotion and waited in a panic for Marvin's reaction.

After a few moments, Marvin came in and walked right past Isobel. He began riffling through the Yellow Pages. He picked up the phone. "Hello, Dr. Kologna? I have a problem with a sick animal. Could you come right over? . . . Can you recommend someone who does make house calls? Nobody? . . . No, I can't wrap him up and bring him over, he's a horse. No, I haven't got a horse transport, it was shortsighted of me. . . . Okay, thanks. I'm at One-twenty Horace Harding Lane." When Marvin got off the phone he walked back and forth aimlessly but quickly, like a caged wildcat, his Hush Puppies squeaking slightly each time he turned. He seemed suddenly more human, more approachable. She offered him a cocktail and he accepted, looking at her as if he hadn't seen her in a long time. He seemed more calm and sat down with his Dewar's on the rocks.

"What's wrong?" she asked.

"The horse is sick," answered Marvin. "He just lies there."

"Maybe he's just resting."

"No, I can tell it's not that. He doesn't want to eat or look at me or anything. I've never seen him like this. His lethargy is beyond lethargy."

"Is the vet coming?"

"The vet doesn't make house calls, but he's sending over a special Long Island horse doctor. That vet I called doesn't do horses, anyway. He specializes in gerbils with goiter."

Isobel laughed. At least he was capable of joking. The bell rang. Isobel looked out the window and saw a large truck. She wondered whether they had a towing charge. She waited inside, staring at the vet's truck in the dusk, wishing the picture window faced the back, and then swishing her drink back and forth over the ice until it looked like rapids. She watched the vet get into the truck without the horse, hoisting himself into the high seat. She heard the motor, and was still staring out when Marvin came in.

"He says he can't find anything wrong. It looks like exhaustion to him." Marvin blushed.

"But you hardly ride him," said Isobel.

"But when I do, we ride far," said Marvin. "Besides, who knows what he does during the day. Maybe he moves around a lot in the garage."

Isobel wondered whether he suspected, but doubted it. Like a child, he was making a quick, unlikely alibi. It was nice to be able to talk to him again.

She waited a week before going to see the horse again. It was a bright day, and cooler. Isobel was fully dressed. Although her appearance was calculated to please the horse, she had no intention of initiating anything, still fearing for the horse's health. She pulled up the door. The place seemed neater. Marvin must have cleaned up. The horse was standing so that she got a complete sideways view of him. He turned his head toward her slowly, with a gaze so large that there seemed to be nothing in the garage but the horse's eyes; still they showed no sign of emotion, surprise, or happiness. She watched his pupils contract with the light. For a moment she considered leaving, then she saw—the horse's penis beginning to move out of its velvet sheath, like an eyeglass case with a tiny beard, and she watched it tumesce slowly, like a Wonderbubbles plastic balloon, and as if by Pavlovian signal, she experienced a surge of warmth and desire, bringing back all her old feelings of previous days. She moved farther inside, rolled the door down behind her, and began to remove her clothes, the horse licking and sniffing her impatiently. So he had missed her! Yes, yes, as she felt and smelled him she realized how much she'd missed him. They patted and licked each other in a frenzy, the horse's fat, flat tongue pressing her breasts, as she lay down on one of the blankets that Marvin had washed and folded in

203

an excess of hygienic zeal. She felt the sensation in her nipples spread all over her body like instant non-dairy Cremora in a cup of hot coffee. Still, he continued licking her breasts and nothing else until she became frantic, then angry. Was he teasing her? She expected to see a smile on his face, but she saw only his eyes and his breathing was so heavy that miniature drops of moisture shot from his nose when he exhaled. He continued to stand over her that way, looking at her, until she couldn't stand it any longer and straddled him from underneath, her arms and legs around his sides and back. She hung there under him, belly to belly, a cool breeze washing over her exposed vagina. As she clung like an infant marsupial, she could feel the tip of his penis. As she edged herself farther back on the horse, still hanging there, he thrust forward and inserted the very tip of his penis. She tried, but couldn't move any further back and the horse seemed to enjoy teasing her. Then, as she was becoming angry again, he thrust forward and filled her, ever more, with his enormous organ, and held still. As she let out a deep moan, the garage door rolled up. Looking almost black with the late-afternoon sun behind him creating a sharp brightness around his ominous body, stood Marvin. For a moment there was total silence, nothing moved. His hand still on the handle of the door, he remained outside and rolled it down. Instead of disembarking from the horse, she surprised herself by continuing to make love with him more passionately than ever before, with an excess of abandon coupled with a sense of doom that drove her even faster, and she and the horse made the most violent love until both of them, lathered with sweat, came, her high-pitched shout mingling with his deep unearthly hoot, and, limp, she dropped off of him. Lying there under him, she saw that he had a line of hair down the center of his underbelly, sticking out, like the waves at Coney Island, when, going in opposite directions, they meet and crest. She stroked the length of it gently and then felt his long, soft penis,

204

which hung there, very long, but soft, like the plastic liner of an Evenflo Nurser when it's three-quarters full of milk, one drop hanging from the tip. Then she let go of it, wiped her legs, and put on her clothes. She kissed the horse on both eyes and left. Marvin never mentioned anything.

The next day, arriving home in time to make Marvin's dinner, she thought she saw the horse standing on the front lawn. Marvin was nowhere in sight. Wondering, she walked faster until she was standing on the neatly shaved lawn next to the horse, who hadn't moved a hair. Looking closer, she noticed that his eyes seemed to be marbles, looking at nothing. She put down her Ohrbach's and Korvette's bags and boxes, leaning them against the horse's stiff leg so that they wouldn't spill, and felt the horse. He was hard as a rock. Leaving her bundles there, she ran back to the garage and found no horse. The garage had been cleaned, and she could almost believe there hadn't been a horse there if it weren't for the blankets still piled in the corner and still smelling of horse. She went to get her packages and felt the horse again. It was stuffed. Marvin met her in the foyer with a vermouth on the rocks with two cherries. She looked at the horse through the picture window while they had their cocktails.

ST. ZITA'S

The wind is blowing through my ears, not roughly,
but gently swirling around and around like a touch I
long to feel, a gentle brush of love along some part of
my flesh, like a warm nose, a worn finger. Is it any
touch or only the essence of Father Sullivan I long
to feel inside me like the wind, rustling the curtains
of this small recording booth. A tiny light is flashing
on and off, under it, the word BEGIN in black letters,
now a small red warning light to the left. My tension
squeezes the moisture from my body in a glow of heat
and the perspiration drips from my lips, muffling my
voice as if it were coming from underwater. So pressed,
I'm at a loss for the important thing I should say, but
automatically a song emerges from me:

> Oh say can you see
> by the dawn's early light
> what so proudly we hailed
> those amber waves of grain
> for purple mountains majesty
> O'er the twilight's last gleaming.
> O beautiful for spacious skies
> And the rocket's red glare
> the bombs bursting in air
> across the fruited plain.
> America, America
> gave proof through the night

God shed his grace on thee
and crown thy good
with brotherhood
and proudly doth wave
from sea to shiny sea
o'er the homes of the brave and
the land of the free.

Tears and perspiration mingled on my upper lip in a
sudden wave ready to overflow. A tiny dial says ONE
MINUTE MORE, but I've finished, and when the lights
go out a slot vomits a small record at me, already
wrapped, to keep forever. I slip it between my breasts
like a coin in a candy machine but, out of order, it
remains there, while I float into another booth, which,
as I look into a mirror, I find that five pictures of me
have been taken and spat out in a white folder. One
in surprise at finding myself looking at me in this
small booth, curtain still rustling from my entrance.
Two, removing a small black seed from between two
teeth, three, my mouth spread all over my face, contracting everything else into a wrinkled frame as I
examine the overall teeth for more seeds. Number
four is my eyes, trying to look up while I hold my
head down and scrape a few dandruff flakes away
from an area near my forehead, and five is just a bunch
of my hair as I've bent over to shake a lot of dandruff
out. Some white flakes show like snow, as my hair
has photographed darker than it usually is. Altogether
I feel that they aren't representative of me, but neither
is my own body, which, bloated rancid and yellow, is
like a vinyl covering over me, loosely blown up, and
if I had the courage I would slit it one day with a
knife from top to bottom, and the real me would step
out, thin and firm, glowing with integrity, beauty. But
I'm a coward. I accept what each day brings, or what
it takes.

As I lie here on my mat, under the sign MADONNA,
THE GIRL WITH THE TWITCHING CUNT, a large, provocative poster that certainly doesn't look like me,

except for the breasts, and there is a vague resemblance in the eyes, which are the same eyes as on the Lord Jesus as he hangs from his cross in full color above my head, I think how he suffered for my sins. But I suffer for his sins, I think, as a man dressed as a doctor rolls in on flat feet and takes a hypodermic out of a black bag. It's filled with tiny candy pills of all colors, and in one moment they are gone and I feel them popping silently in my body. They're similar to the ones Blaise used to press to my arm in the center of my vaccination, like a rocket reaching the moon, the plastic touch with no reaction. I much preferred the plastic thermometer, first up my ass, then hers. But when that's lost, a pencil or something else will do. I don't trust that doctor, but I have no choice. I know he's only dressed as a doctor, he's really someone else, masquerading. What he is I don't know, but I'm at his mercy. As soon as I can get up, I'll return to the recording booth. I'll wait till the light says BEGIN, then I'll tell the story of my life, on an installment of I don't know how many records. Perhaps they'll be reviewed in the Literary Supplement of the Sunday *Times*. I've just seen a roach jump out of its skin, so white, pale, and vulnerable, leaving his empty crusty shell behind, he hurries to join the others marching in formation along the cracks in the floor; but I don't try to kill them, not only because it's useless but because they look like armies, soldiers marching in defense of themselves, and I have respect for soldiers and armies, especially since I'm unable to defend myself. Even though it's warm and balmy in this tent where my mat is, I know it's New Year's Eve. I can hear Guy Lombardo and his orchestra playing faintly, though I don't know where it's coming from. It's probably piped in as one of our special services. No one wants to lose them. A Girl With a Twitching Cunt is not a common phenomenon, and people come to me from far and wide. Why the manager gets paid and not me is beyond me, but every time I've tried to go into business for myself, someone steps in to collect the money. But at least I get a steady

208

salary, and I don't have to worry about a thing. I get my feedings through the vein, it keeps me going, and I have this mat, leather or plastic, I can't tell anymore, but it's softer than the butcher's block I had before. All this is the will of God anyway. Next to my rosary given to me by Father Sullivan is my tiny bronze medal with the words, half embossed, half engraved: CHRISTIAN GIRL OF THE YEAR. Life seemed so promising when I went up onto the stage in Father Sullivan's magnificent church to receive it, and as I walked off the other side I got a pinch on my ass but not from Father Sullivan, whose virtue wouldn't allow him to touch me or any other girl. I've actually received no other medal. That was my only reward for being a good Christian, and it's kept me going ever since. I'm getting sleepy. There've been no customers for a long time.

Father Sullivan is coming to me again, sneaking in through the west flap, no no, climbing through the top where there is a little niche of sky sliding through, spreading around in here, bringing its warm blue odor, and Father Sullivan's odor, of which he has many, some are imagined, compiled of certain real odors I have possessed and saved forever to use again and again. As I wrap Father Sullivan in his odors and mine, I draw him to me, holding his hovering face before me with my hot breath, his nose just touches mine, his gaze has blurred, soon I'll feel his lips, I am limp and as open as a hamburger patted flat—no, no, it's too fast. To prolong it, I send him back, he'll have to begin again, slower. It's his back, hairless and slender but firm and smooth, that I'm feeling now. I'm kissing his slender ribs, who knows where his legs are, I'm not caressing those yet, perhaps they're out across me like a cross, perhaps they're over my head, or leaning against a wall. I cannot be aware of his whole body at once since I concentrate on one thing at a time, it's enlarged, we are enlarged and absorbed. Now my face is being absorbed into his face, slightly oily nose grazing my eye, lips all over me at once, tongues

pressed together like snails on glass, eyelashes clasped
—no, no, not so quickly again. He's leering above me,
face close but not touching, his gentle fingers are firmly
holding the lips of my cunt apart till I'm nothing but
a waiting hole, open, anything in the room might be
sucked into that vacuum, but that cock, large and
poised, purple and smooth, almost touching, resists,
while I lie still, then, my body writhing unsuccessfully
to scoop him in, I kiss a smooth upper arm, and gently
grab two furred balls. Suddenly I'm filled to the top
by something curved like a pumpkin stem that emits
sparks sometimes but now lies there quiet and heavy,
pressing all my organs away, still and heavy like a
balloon filled with water, which suddenly bursts. Father
Sullivan flies, out through the top of the tent again,
and I'm left on this mat, torpid and repentant. Everything seems meaningless, including writing this, which
cannot express what I want to say, but seems to run
along parallel to my thoughts, close, but never merging
to become one with them. All this jabbering makes me
ill, so I have two New Year's resolutions:
    1. I will not write this anymore.
    2. I will never again imagine I am making love with
Father Sullivan.

I'm lying on my stomach naked and I feel a hand
caress my back, which sends a beautiful chill through
my whole body. I lie still while echoes of the chill
repeat themselves and I dare not move. Someone with
a very gentle finger is tracing the whole poem "How
Do I Love Thee" by Elizabeth Barrett Browning, letter
by letter on my ass, while I become mesmerized. I'm
spread out on my stomach like a bear rug, melting into
the floor, when I feel someone's teeth biting into the
back of my neck like a male cat mounting a female,
while a cock gently slips in between my almost closed
legs, remaining like that for a moment. Suddenly I
feel a whole body weight on my back—I can't go on.
See, I told you, I couldn't make any resolutions. I
haven't kept any. Somebody is coming. I see shined

210

black shoes, blue socks with tiny American flags sewn
on where the anklebone protrudes, and the bottom of
a night stick. Policemen are the only ones who don't
pay. I retain my virtue by not paying any attention to
what I'm doing. When the policeman mounts me with
nothing on but his American-flag socks, neatly cuffed
down, I don't see him, I don't feel him. He shouts,
"Twitch it tighter, baby!" I close my cunt tight around
something, I'm not sure what, perhaps a night stick, as
I'm pounded in mechanical rhythm, to which I say
nursery rhymes to myself: PEASE porridge HOT
pease PORridge COLD pease PORRIDGE in the POT
NINE days OLD. I've been used, wrapped around
someone's rod like a plastic bag to be filled with goldfish and tadpoles, and who's more virtuous than I?
I've never even used contraceptives. I've given birth
to thousands of children, all stillborn at one month.

Father Sullivan is pure, that's probably why I love
him. I search for purity day and night. Although I've
defiled my image most disgracefully by doing everything
in my power to seduce him, like Jesus Himself, he
remains pure. How he's resisted my seductions is
nothing short of a miracle since I've demanded nothing
in return, yet he's never put a finger on me. "Through
me you will remain pure," he always said. Someone is
kissing my stomach and pulling my pubic hair hard, but
it doesn't hurt, it's Father Sullivan, who is wearing his
black suit, his pants pulled down just below the buttocks, who brings in with his white sneakers the sweaty
odor of the church where we all lived, especially the
game room with the shiny floors, the bingo room where
all the women were naked, their asses reflecting the
beautiful stained-glass windows, recalling Fridays and
Tuesdays when I sat under the buffet, dragging down
and consuming heavy, fragrant-moist rum cake baked
and donated by volunteers. The room would spin
slightly and I never achieved my ambition to turn the
bingo cage and call softly the numbers, as Father
Sullivan did, who was my foster father then after
mother was arrested for prostitution and gambling. She

was only arrested for a few days, but while she was in jail an agent of the CIA discovered that there was a cache of marijuana in her cunt. She was given thirty years for possession. Father Sullivan had custody of me and Blaise at that time. Beautiful Blaise, who was named after Father Sullivan's favorite philosopher, Blaise Pascal, whose image often merged with my memories of Father Sullivan until I don't know which is which, for when I've made love with Father Sullivan, and have been absorbed into his blue eyes and held up in the air by his thin arms, I realize afterward that Father Sullivan's eyes are brown and it was Blaise's eyes and Blaise's smooth wet tongue that had touched only my nipple tips, while Father Sullivan's thick, strong, short-fingered hands that had held me up by my waist, just grazing my rib cage, were attached to blond Blaise's thin arms, elbows flaring out a bit to the right and the left like her precious knees. I've never had a room as beautiful and as magnificent as the one Blaise and I shared in the church while we were the Ten-Year-Old Virgins of Our Lady, Most Precious Virgin Mother of Our Lord of the Most Sacred Blood, Martyr Forever. My mat crackles slightly as if the leather is all dry, or perhaps it is plastic that causes it to crackle, though one excellent thing about our technology in this country we can be thankful for, one proof, is the ability to make plastic look so much like leather that it's impossible to tell the difference. Perhaps this mat is filled with straw, although I was promised cotton. I do my job. When they say, "Tighter," I squeeze my cunt as tight as I can. I can twitch it sixteen times in quick succession.

My two ambitions are:
  1. To be able to twitch my cunt twenty times in quick succession.
  2. To be good.

Blaise and I had a lovely room in the church. We were nine then and I still blush when I think that Father

Sullivan lied about our age when he said we were ten. And though I remember masturbating as I gazed blearily at a larger-than-life-size statue of Jesus on the Cross, concentrating equally on his sensuous look of pain, which could be pleasure, and his sculptured genitals, with even the hair artistically molded out of plaster, resembling the waves of the sea lapping about the mast of his cock, and embossed with gold leaf. I can hardly remember any of those people who came to our room. It is their singsong moans I recall, wordless incomprehensible sounds bringing tears of sympathy to my eyes, all varieties of sounds I would wish to be incorporated in the recording of my life, some of them actually incorporating my name Ohhh—Ma——don ———aaaaaaaa, or Madonn-aaaaaaaaa

na.

o

don

or Ma

Nor do I recall their cocks, but I do recall their Oh Henrys, their Fifth Avenue bars, their Black Crows and Ju Jubes, their Powerhouses. Those Clark bars, always crisp, always erect, till the last mouthful. That's when I learned how to twitch my cunt, lying on the bed or on the floor, my eyes never leaving the candy that lay on the tiny triangular table that fit into the corner so nicely, just the front legs bulging with varicose adornment. I could rid myself of the writhing weight in less than five seconds (one mississippi, two mississippi) and the tighter I twitched, the fewer seconds, until I was hardly down, Blaise standing over us watching, drooling on us, waiting to share my candy. Then I was up, opening the candy, picnicking on an absorbent towel, my client either buttoning his pants or lying where I left him, in a state of lethargy bordering on idiocy, his member limp and glistening. Blaise's clients usually preferred to jerk off while she danced, and she, moving her slender hips, and cupping breasts that didn't exist, twirled and writhed in response to their "Faster, faster," as their veins swelled, lying there like

213

blimps, jowls straining, till the fountain burst over their hot fingers still wrapped around their cocks—sometimes the index finger of the other hand simultaneously up their ass—milky fluid resting in bellybuttons and filling the spaces between pubic hairs like the bubbles in a plastic wand before it's blown into. Even at that time I had fantasies of Father Sullivan, though more than ever I pictured him with a body like Jesus, a cock, chocolate-covered and erect, pimpled with unseen nuts like an Oh Henry, or embossed with chocolate stripes, or bulging with three almonds in a row like an Almond Joy, and as I see my mouth ready to receive him I can still taste the chocolate, the chocolate which I can never brush from my teeth, which was already beginning to rot my body even then, from the inside out. Could I help it if my small rounded nipples grew large and dark, and my breasts rose from underneath like volcanoes out of the sea? Was it caused by my filthy fantasies of Father Sullivan which I didn't dare to confess to him? Although Blaise gazed at my breasts with envy, her light finger with its dirty fingernail gently and abstractedly following the light blue veins like a car traveling around a mountain to the summit, Father Sullivan shrank from the sight of them in disgust.

Slowly I rise on my mat, first propping my upper torso with my elbow and turning till I'm on my left side, then crossing my legs under me, I'm up in a flash without even the help of my arms. No, that's a lie. One resolution I must make is never to lie. First I turn over on my mat, to my side, where I wait for a moment for all the fat to turn. When my whole body is still once again, I turn onto my stomach, where, buried in flesh, I attempt to crawl blindly, by pulling up my knees to my head and moving along like an inch-worm. Off my mat, my head's in the sawdust now and I'm groping for something to pull myself upright on, perhaps I'm approaching a chair. I'm going for a walk, perhaps back to the recording booth, but it will soon be time for my shot. A premonitory feeling of panic as I picture the hypodermic wielder arriving and not finding me at home, on my mat. Then I see me, rushing back from a walk I haven't taken, finding the needle bearer gone. I view these scenes with a sense of tragedy far deeper than even after I've completed my affairs with Father Sullivan, and he has disappeared, either he or I saying good night, or neither saying anything, when an instant of reality intervenes, bringing with it a sense of despair. When I return from my walk, I'll do my exercises. These are to strengthen me so that one day I can eventually leave this place and search for Father Sullivan, to whom something horrible must have happened or I'd never have been left in that horrible place. I also want to become sleek and slender for him. I've resolved to do those exercises for years now. Perhaps Father Sullivan is dead now, I really must go look for him, but I'm afraid to be gone too long. I feel something with the knuckles of my hand, buried in sawdust. I grope higher, hold on, and raise my head. It is a barstool, and if I'm careful I can raise myself to an upright position with its support, without throwing it over on me. I carefully place one hand on a rung and the other hand on an opposite rung, and though the stool rocks back and forth I'm up. I brush back my hair, casually, as if it were absolutely no effort for me to move about, as if there were no perspiration on my upper lip, my nose and forehead, and dripping between my breasts. I feel the edge of my ear as I do so, enlarged from genitals being inserted into it, as all my orifices are, my nostrils included, my navel, abused, and my mouth, no longer able to close, completely retains a circular shape of surprise, with the tip of my tongue peering out like a clitoris. It isn't in this place that I was abused like that. Father Sullivan was no longer there when I undressed with the others in the back room and had a card tied around my waist with the number 679 on it. I tried to see some significance in that number and I couldn't, but I know the significance existed whether I discover it or not.

"Number six-seven-nine, how much am I bid?"

yelled someone, as I was thrust naked onto a wooden platform. In front of me was a crowd of people on bridge chairs. I can recall the pain in my bare feet from the splinters, which were removed later by someone who bid eighty-seven cents a pound for me. The madam carefully picked out all the wood from my tender soles with a needle, the tip blackened by a match. It was at her funeral, under the eye of Walter B. Cook, in a simple mahogany casket with a beautiful mauve velvet lining (quilted), that I first saw her dressed. That's the day I saw St. Zita's. Shall I tell about St. Zita's? No, that would jinx it for me. I made a vow never to tell about St. Zita's.

Okay, I'll tell about St. Zita's. You see, I can't keep a vow. I was saving St. Zita's as a last chance for me. Even my telling about St. Zita's proves my unworthiness. No, I won't tell. Is it possible I'm becoming stronger? More virtuous? Can I recall the Pledge of Allegiance? Which hand goes over the heart? Which side is the heart on again? What if my heart is on the right side instead of the left? Houdini's appendix was on the left side instead of the right. As long as I'm out, I'll visit Father Sullivan. The moment I think the name "Father Sullivan" I see him walk by abstracted, but when he sees my shoes, my ankle, something about my ankle reminds him of me, whom he has missed all these years. I stop, knowing he'll look up, tentatively waiting for his eyes to travel up from my tiny little anklebone, over my calf, and the underside of my knee, where pale veins play tautly, and my kneecap, which gently smiles its little cupid face at him, and—instant recognition.

"Madonna?"

I smile shyly, heart beating hard, pumping blood into my face and behind my glowing eyes, turning on their sensuous signal lights. There's great love coming into his face, deep love, like Clark Gable, but a deep speechless youthful innocent, incomprehensible little-boy love

216

like James Dean, but neat, clean, like Gregory Peck, but gentle and creasy like Marcello Mastroianni,

"How I've missed you, Madonna, every moment. Have I ever stopped thinking about you?" I stand there, incandescent, with a face like Silly Putty, afraid to admit the same.

"Madonna, I will not live without you for another moment. Go get your things and come live with me in the church. I'll walk you back to get your things." He takes my arm and drags my Silly Putty feet along until we are directly in front of a red triangle, a bold bikini from which pour two massive, white gummy thighs composed of 8,000,000000000,0000 airbrush dots, above which is a black navel maelstrom and when one emerges from that, one sees them overhead, Mount Everest and Etna, ready to erupt, separated by the Grand Canyon, and a bit uneven, as if alongside the San Andreas fault, and above that a floating smile, resembling no one's in the world, but just a little bit, by a few mere molecules, a bit resembling mine, Madonna, the Girl With the Twitching Cunt, a red-lipped Wrigley's Spearmint Juicy Fruit coffee-break airbrush smile. Father Sullivan is pale, a piece of crumpled paper, not wanting to litter yet not knowing where to throw himself, and from his mouth floats a whisper, "You've been fucked." Oh, it's no use. I'm so useless. Yet I remember it, I've just remembered it—the Pledge of Allegiance, I mean:

> I pledge allegiance
> to the flag
> of the United States of America
> and to the republic
> for which it stands
> one nation, under God, indivisible
> with liberty and justice for all.

As long as I can still remember the pledge, I can still allow myself to consider myself a candidate for St. Zita's. I can still remember the madam, in her dress, lying in the casket like a doll with heavy makeup, as she'd always worn heavy makeup. Walter Cook, who understands, didn't put on the madam's makeup the way she did, but the shocking thing that I noticed was that the madam in death was like an object, her body lying there in a repose similar to sleep, yet far from sleep, even a sleep where no breathing is visible, the evidence of life was never so tangible as when I was confronted by death. The madam might as well have been a table. And I further blasphemed by daydreaming to the extent that I missed the services and the prayers, a private discourse with myself about whether or not it would've been more fitting to have the madam lying naked in the casket, and buried naked, perhaps with just a pair of her high heels, maybe the snakeskin ones she always wore or just the new trowel-toed ones. Oh, I'm so sick—perhaps if I never saw St. Zita's I could be happy, but I can't help desiring to be there. When I left the madam's funeral, everything was gray outside, there was a slight mist, like rain, but it wasn't falling, it was incorporated in the air. I opened my black umbrella, but the moisture came under it, filled it. I was annoyed that my sculpted and dyed beehive hairdo was going to be invaded and fall. I suddenly felt a beautiful feeling, that the rain was beautiful. I was beautiful even with my beehive dented, the gray was beautiful, the sidewalk, the sky, the houses, the mist, the air. There was a beautiful little gray tree behind a little gray gate, no leaves, then a gray house with a flat facade, and a small American flag protruding above an engraved medallion. I read it. It said ST. ZITA'S HOME FOR FRIENDLESS WOMEN.

"Thank you, O Lord," I wept, "for this revelation." Who was more friendless than I? But naturally I didn't go in. I wanted to become worthy first. That was seven years ago. But I will when I can keep my resolutions. Then when I ring the bell at St. Zita's, a gentle woman looking a bit like Blaise, but aged, will take me in her arms and show me a simple clean room, and I'll live with those saintly women and perhaps be saintly myself.

Really, if I want to get back on my mat I must hurry. I'm beginning to feel sick already and the fear of being sick is rushing the symptoms. But I think mother is in here. I have a feeling she is, if I can find the entrance. By now I've been around the building two and a half times, crawling like a worm and feeling everywhere, and have found no entrance at all. But here's a large slit, surely they didn't just leave these spaces for nothing. I squeeze myself head first into the dark space. There isn't even enough room to light a match. I'm able to imagine myself as Father Sullivan's cock, squeezing itself into somewhere, my head feels bald, with a tiny slit on top, but no, I see a light, it's more like being born. I try to push myself farther, but I'm unsuccessful, until someone takes me by the head and pulls, and sets me on my feet without even glancing back. He resumes pacing the small room we're in. I get on a line of people all of whom are waiting to see a man in a little booth. I went over to the policeman who pulled me in and I asked him what the line was for.

"You have to wait on it to find out. Have your identification ready," he warned me.

"What sort?"

"Do you have a driver's license, or a library card?"

Oh, no, I thought, but I just went on line and didn't say a word. Next to the booth was a large frame on a stand with a saying in large black letters: A STITCH IN TIME SAVES NINE, and above that, a shelf with some gears, some leather key chains, some license plates, and three paper dolls which were dusty and folding over, with another framed sign, but small, that said MADE BY THE INMATES OF THE HOUSE OF DETENTION.

"Who are you visiting?" asked the officer in the booth.

"My mother."

"Name?"

"Mary Magdalene Flanagan."

219

gan, Mary Magdalene Flanagan, here we are." He fished a card out of his files.

"I have to see whether your mother has listed you as a visitor," he said. "Yes, here you are, Madonna Flanagan. Identification please." He is looking searchingly at me.

"But I don't have any, I forgot my purse," I tell him.

"I'm sorry, but the rule is I have to see some identification."

Panicking now, because I want to see my mother, and I must have already missed my injection anyway, I lift my skirt and show him a birthmark on my upper thigh. I don't want him to see the lash marks that reside a little farther up. He is thinking for a moment, he can't decide whether that constitutes identification, then he writes a number on a yellow slip of paper, hands it to me, and says, "Okay." I'm ready to go over to the large gate, when behind the officer I catch a glimpse of someone. I feel about ready to faint.

"Who is that?" I whispered.

"That's Father Sullivan," he answers impatiently, and I'm shoved aside by the person next in line. Perhaps inside I'll see him, it must be him, I'm sure. How I long to see him and yet how I hate for him to see me yet. I'm not myself yet, I'm still evil and ugly. Oh, I see him, he's seen me through the window of the booth and now he's coming to get me, is having the gates opened. We just stare at each other for a few moments, his eyes devour me until I'm small and delicate, then they pick me up and carry me to a small cell, where he silently removes my clothes and gently traces all my scars and every spot on my body with the tips of all his fingers. First my hair and cheeks, as I lie there face down, then my neck and hair, then the top of my back, the middle of my back, and the side of my breast, the gently tracing finger producing a slightly different sensation on different areas until, by the time his fingers reach my waist, which is different front and back, and which I love perhaps best of all, I'm jarred from my uterine stupor by a buzzing, which is the electrical opening of the gate, slowly sliding into heaven knows where so slowly that it's at least five minutes before the opening is large enough for me to fit through, then a small corridor and another gate which doesn't open untill the first gate is closed, leaving me in between for a moment as if I'm caught in the game of London Bridge. I give a guard at a desk my yellow slip, and he points to a corridor.

"The women are that way," he says. I walk until I come to a room full of people each next to a little glass window, each talking into a telephone attached to the side of the window. Was I assigned a window and don't know which? If I pick a window, will she find me on the other side? I'm feeling quite sick now, perspiration dripping between my breasts down into my waistband in spite of the fact that I'm cold, and again consider running back to my mat, but I'm paralyzed at the thought of the rigmarole for getting out of here. Perhaps when I leave here I'll go to St. Zita's, I think, but will they, when they come to answer the door in their chignons and brown uniforms, something like Brownie uniforms, only with long skirts, will they say, "You can't come in here, you dirty ugly, vile woman"? Because if they say that, what then? I look again for mother behind the windows and I see—yes, it is—Father Sullivan, giving chocolate bars to the inmates, and then I see mother looking for me, but no tears fill her eyes. I can see her lips screaming at me, but I can't hear, I'm afraid that the phone won't work. She's gesticulating wildly and pointing to another window. This time the phone works but with a painful static. Nevertheless, I hear mother yelling at me for not having come before. She's been here twenty-five years, and her case hasn't come to trial yet. Of course she's senile, she's not the mother I knew, but an ancient piece of flesh like something spilled and left to harden. She's so short she can barely reach the window. Inside her head there's a vacuum cleaner sucking in her mouth, lips, and eyes, trying desperately for her chin, her nose, succeeding only in bending them toward each other.

"How are you?" I scream.

"How do you expect?" she yells. "How are you?"

"I'm fine, mother, I'm married to a lawyer," I tell her, "and we have two beautiful children and a house."

"Wonderful," she says. "Then you were right to stay away from here." Then her eyes look behind her while her head stays in the same position, and she whispers, "Be careful what you say, these phones are bugged." I lean on the window frame, feeling too sick to stand.

"Did I ever tell you how father died?" she asks in a whisper. "He swallowed a roach."

"What do you mean?" I ask incredulously.

"The butt of a pot cigarette. One night we were smoking and there was a very tiny end left and your father always liked to smoke it way down, sometimes burning his fingers or lips, and I told him, 'One day you're going to suck that butt all the way in and choke to death.' Well, one night he inhaled and never exhaled again. I called for an ambulance, and I couldn't get a dial tone, and then the emergency number was busy, so I called the operator and she was very nice. By the time the ambulance arrived, Harry was swollen and blue. They took X-rays of his lungs and when they saw the roach there they didn't know what jurisdiction he came under, the hospitals or the courts. They tried to measure the amount of pot your father had on him by measuring the roach in the X-rays with calipers, and by the time they decided what to do, Harry was black with white fingertips and floating two feet above the X-ray table."

"Time's up," said someone, and a guard on the other side took my mother by the elbow. And again, behind them I saw Father Sullivan, but I didn't know how to get his attention. I scream into the phone, which is shut off, and he can't hear me at all. I scream louder and I can't even hear myself scream. I don't want to wake up because I feel my cunt twitching, but not just that, then my uterus twitches, then my rectum and

my intestines and my stomach, and my heart and my
bladder and urethra and kidneys in a giant orgasm that
turns my body inside out so that the air is very painful
to my organs, unprojected as they are by any skin,
and directly above my head I become aware of a
brown circle, edged in scarlet, now changing to orange,
and yellow, like the lights in a jukebox, and I realize
that it's an eye looking at me with such cold objective
curiosity that I'm frightened out of my wits, and skin-
less me would like to sink into oblivion, but some sadist
is calling, "Madonna, Madonna, Madonna, Madonna,
Madonna, Madonna.

"Madonna, you can't stay here. Madonna, get up,
you have to get out."

"But, Father, I'm sick—where can I go? I can't
get up. . . ."

"Meet me at the church. I have to stay here for a
while. I'd like to help you, Madonna, but I'd rather
not touch you. It's your fault for getting yourself into
this mess." With a rag that was lying on the bed he
lifted me and helped me off the bed. I began crawling.
He held the door to the cell open for me and I followed
him down the corridors, crawling, and felt the cold
air on my wet body as he let me out into the yard where
the police vans were and the buses. I don't know how
long I crawled along the yard. Perhaps I lost consciousness, for I wasn't aware of anything until I felt
myself being wrapped in cotton gently, perhaps to be
tucked in a warm box somewhere, but no, it was
someone wrapping his jacket around me, gently, but
efficiently, making a neat package. I hear the words
"Don't scream" whispered into my ear, before the
collar goes up around my head and buttons somewhere
over my eyes. I feel a button like a third eye in the
middle of my forehead, but through a tiny opening I
see the officer with his pants down around the middle
of his thighs, like someone standing in water, his member stiff and steaming in the cold. Now it's dark, as
the edges close around my eyes. Why would I scream?
I don't even think of screaming, I'm like a sperm cell

in a wad of semen. I don't know what he has planned to do to me, what he's done, I haven't felt a thing, and I don't even feel that sort of thing anymore. I'm being alternately dragged and carried, then thrown into what seems to be a car or vehicle of some sort.

"Can I give you a lift?"

"Would you take me to our Lady, Most Precious Virgin Mother of Our Lord of the Most Sacred Blood, Martyr Forever Church, please," I ask in a muffled voice from deep inside the jacket that's wrapped around me.

"Sure, lady." When we get there, he removes me from the car, lays me on the ground, still in the jacket, and rolls me off in the direction of the church door.

"Toodle-oooo," he calls.

I ring the bell at the side of the church, but no one answers. Well, I know of another entrance, through the church. The only reason I'm here now is to confess before I die, because I've never been so sick. I'm crawling down the aisle past people praying in some of the pews, praying so hard that they don't even see me crawling by. Now I must be a sight and I know for sure Father Sullivan will be disgusted by me, for now, soft and limp, moist and warm, loose and languid, I leak down the aisle toward the altar, passing over a floor colored with the reflections from the stained-glass windows, now red, now gold, then a bit of orange, now blue, and I'm almost to the little door, the inside door to Father Sullivan's quarters.

"Father, Father," I shout in a hoarse whisper.

Someone sitting nearby knocked on the door for me and said, "Father, someone wants to have confession."

Father Sullivan came to the door. I saw only his sneakers as he answered, "Confession is on Wednesday and Monday—oh, it's you, you certainly are persevering, aren't you? Well, crawl on in."

"Please, Father, can I stay here for a while? I'm sick and I can't make it back to where I live, my boss will yell at me for leaving, maybe he'll beat me."

"You're an addict, aren't you, Madonna?"

224

"Oh yes, but I'm kicking it, that's why I'm sick."

"That's disgusting, Madonna, I won't have anything to do with addicts, they have no conscience. I'm a man of God."

"But Jesus teaches us to help others, Father."

"God helps those who help themselves."

"But, Father, please, I love you so, I've always loved you."

"What you mean by love is not the kind I believe in."

"What do you mean?"

"You believe in carnal love and I in spiritual love."

"But I do love you spiritually, I do, I love you almost the way I love Jesus."

"That's blasphemy. You must go now. A rolling stone gathers no moss."

"I will go, just confess me now, please, because I want to begin fresh, start all over, please, please, please, please, please . . ."

"Okay, just don't get too close," said Father Sullivan, moving off. I followed him into the bathroom. He opened the shower curtain, stepped into the tub, and pulled the curtain closed.

I began, "Bless me, Father, for I have sinned."

"Go on, go on, be specific."

"Oh, I can't, I'm just so ashamed—Go on? Well, even regarding you, I've desired you carnally rather than spiritually, I curse, use the name of the Lord in vain, I've coveted you, I've dreamed of you twenty-four hours a day, violating every part of my body in every imaginable way, I'm an addict and a prostitute, and I even use contraception. . . ."

"Wait, wait," said Father Sullivan, "be more specific, describe the way you imagine me violating you, start at the beginning and let me have details."

"Well . . ." I knew it was blasphemous of me, but perhaps it was something in Father Sullivan's voice, something familiar, but I did so much want to see him in there, to see his face, perhaps to find if there was any sign of response to me, to what I said . . .

There was a tiny crack where the shower curtain

225

closed in front, but so small that one would have to be at a certain angle in order to see into the tub, so I tried to manipulate myself into that position while still talking, and finally I succeeded. Father Sullivan was on a small wooden stool, leaning back in what seemed to be a very uncomfortable manner. A slight shift again in my position revealed Father Sullivan's pants down around his thighs, pale curly hair, like stockings, ending cleanly at the top of his legs, but erupting into a mass of hair at the base of an erection, around which the pink, stretched tight lips of a kneeling priest went up and down like a machine.

I got out of there as fast as my bloated swollen body could carry its swelling disgust and disillusion. I was pregnant with them, they lay, squirmed, and expanded within me, and somehow I managed to carry them outside the church. I ran down into a subway, but at the bottom of the second landing, feeling at home in the faint odor of urine of the dusty corner, I was violently sick, and vomited, but instead of stopping when there was nothing in my stomach anymore, my whole body slithered out in one long barf and, in an effort to catch my breath, my body went into a jackknife. I can't remember anything much after that. I was vaguely aware of crowds of people passing by, but none of them noticed me or at any rate paid any attention to me there. Perhaps I was there for a few days.

I see Father Sullivan, his head back, veins in his neck protruding and making his delicate neck suddenly thick, his eyes protruding on swivels like a crab, arms out in supplication, fingers lying gently in tiny puddles of water, and his cock with those lips around it . . . and I'm full of desire and excitement. That makes me realize I'm better. But even more, most of all, I desire a shot. But I have no money and no place to go. I could begin again at my old work of hustling, and that's what I really intend to do, but when I get up the stairs, clutching the rail and ascending slowly, while people rush around me, I see it's warm out.

I must have been down there all winter. It's soft out and light, like walking in cotton, next best to floating in amniotic fluid, and I think of St. Zita's again. A place to go, and just as fearful as ever to go there, feeling just as degraded as usual, just by chance at this point my life is such a vacuum that that dream, as a possibility in a lack of possibilities, has the power to move me. I don't know whether it exists anymore, and I'm not quite sure whether it was real, but soon I do see it, the strange gray flatness of it and the plaque: ST. ZITA'S HOME FOR FRIENDLESS WOMEN. I'm applying, and once and for all I qualify. I search for a bell, but all I see is a knocker, austere and brass, which has a rustic sound when I clap it against the heavy door.

"Who is it?"

I don't know what to answer, I feel like a salesman who doesn't want to reveal that he is until the door is opened, and since she doesn't know me, it's useless to say my name. I'm tempted to answer, "me," but at the last moment I feel with chagrin that that kind of coyness is out of place here.

"A friendless woman," I answer, flushing. The door is opened and the sun is shining on the body of a woman wearing nothing at all except a pair of high heels.

"Well, come inside and wait—madam will be back." The slow old door behind me is shut and the last crescent of sunlight is gone from the woman's ass.

SOME DINNERS

We sat across from each other, waiting for our food. I'd ordered scampi to try to avoid becoming obese from having two dinners every night, one with my kids and one with my dates, later. I tried to skip the one with the children, but I never could, I was hungry. He had looked in a scrapbook the waiter had given him wherein were pasted wine labels, and had silently pointed to one. The bottle was now on our table, perspiring coldly. The waiter poured a tiny bit into his glass for him to taste, and stood there, but, unfortunately, Joseph's mouth was full and he was hurrying up to finish chewing all the salad with the watercress and mushrooms blooming out the sides like a cow in pasture. He blushed. We waited, watching him. I wanted to pick up the glass, taste the wine, and nod, but Joseph liked everything done the right way. He gave one last deep swallow where, I thought, with less fortitude he'd have choked, and picked up the glass which I was almost about to down, practically grabbing it from me, glaring at me, and, red-faced, took a sip. He nodded to the waiter, who walked away. I knew he couldn't have really tasted it with the Roquefort dressing still glowing at the corners of his mouth, the Tiffany lamps reflecting off it, outlining his lips with a gleam.

"Would you go with me to a corporation dinner at the Plaza?" he asked. I looked up at him to see whether he was serious. He was breaking up bread and dipping it into the salad dressing. He was always serious.

"You don't know what you'd be getting into," I said. "I'm no good at those kinds of things. I always say the wrong thing."

"Well, I don't think so. It'll be okay."

I knew he either wanted me to come for appearances —though certainly I didn't have the correct appearance—or probably because I was one. of the only women who didn't mind that he was impotent. Well then, did I want to go to a corporation dinner at the Plaza, a fancy place, with fancy stiff people? I don't have any manners. He looked up for the answer. I said yes. It would be interesting. I'd try to have fun. I'd do a research project. I'd talk to the women and find out what it was like to be an executive's wife.

It would be fancy, but I was dressed fancy in my Mick Jagger dress that someone had given me, that he'd worn once in the movie *Performance*, when he was a transvestite. We (Mick Jagger and I) must. be about the same height, so the dress fit perfectly. That kind of dress has to fit perfectly,. because it's a soft gray silky material, gently reaching to the floor, but the arm straps didn't really widen very much as they went down over the breasts, and they never came together in the middle, leaving a wide slit between the breasts that reached directly to the waistband. The only thing that held it on were the breasts themselves, and any movement or twist of the body was extremely scintillating and provoking. I had the mike from my tape recorder under my left breast, and the part with the tape was between my legs. I hoped it wouldn't get screwed up, but I developed an interesting way of walking with my legs apart.

Joseph rang the bell and ran upstairs. He was

nervous because he had a cab waiting and was afraid I'd be late. He was so happy that I was ready on time that he didn't even notice my dress. He attempted to ignore my children because he wanted me to hurry, and it took at least ten minutes to kiss them good night in the doorway, announcing to any neighbor or thief, waiting in the hall until I left, that I was going out. Zach took one last look at my dress and said, "I'm not marrying Juliette anymore, Lynda, I'm going to marry you."

"You can't marry me, Zach."

"Why, Lynda?"

"Because I'm never getting married." I held my hem away from the dusty stairs as we ran down. The top of Joseph's black bow tie was sticking out from under his topcoat.

"It's nice of you to come with me," he said. "I know it'll be a bore, maybe you shouldn't have said yes."

"Oh no," I said, "it'll be fun for me to see one of these affairs. I've made up my mind to enjoy it."

We went up the high marble steps with the stone balustrade surrounding it like a protective fort, walked across miles of red carpet, skirting enormous pillars, seemingly for miles, until, taped to a combination imitation French Empire and Italian Renaissance satin couch we saw a sign: MARROON ROOM—LEFT, RIGHT, LEFT. We walked endlessly, down one corridor, passing through a room where a wedding was taking place, to another corridor, until at the doorway of an enormous room there was a poster with a banner above it, both of them reading ZELLENSDORF CORPORATION. A man with a crew cut, wearing a tuxedo, asked for our tickets. Then he gave us two small signs with pins on the backs, saying MY NAME IS . . . with special gift pens to fill them out with. I didn't have much space on my dress, so I pinned it at my waist. I wanted to pin it on my breast, but I didn't want to call attention to the tape-recorder mike. We'd done a lot of walking

230

down hotel corridors and I hoped the tape wasn't fucked up. Joseph nodded to some of the people we passed, and a hostess appeared from nowhere, like a genie, in a combination waitress-and-Arabian-princess costume, and showed us to one of a hundred round tables, exactly alike, clothed in white, and flowered with weeping orchids just imported on ice from the jungles of South America for this occasion.

"I don't know most of the people here," said Joseph, fingering absently a gold towel around a bottle of champagne that was comfortably ensconced in an embossed silver ice bucket, like a blanketed baby in a buggy. I was about to pour some for myself when a waiter came and grabbed it from me. The men asked Joseph to introduce himself. Every man called out his name and shook Joseph's hand as Joseph repeated every time, "Joseph Wilson, secondary executive in charge of outgoing." The women were introduced as "my wife," or "the little woman." Nobody asked me what I was. I had my credentials on my right and left side under the thin straps of my gray dress. I even rouged the tops of those breasts a bit with gleamy peach blush and gloss, so they glowed in the creamy light of the chandeliers like dried tears. I took my glass of champagne with me and walked around carefully.

"Hello, mmmmmLynda," said a gray-haired man into my name tag. I wished I had it wired so it could answer him.

"That's not my real name," I said. "I'm incognito tonight." And, as he stared, I put my hand to my crotch, pretending to be scratching, and clicked on the tape recorder. "Excuse me," I said, remembering my manners.

"What's that?" he asked with concern, gently pointing to the tape-recorder wire, which looked like a thin umbilicus wending its way downward under the smooth sleekness of the dress.

231

"Oh, that's nothing. It's just a vein that became enlarged when I was pregnant and never went away."

"Is it dangerous?" he asked solicitously.

"Oh, no," I said, "it's nothing. It popped slightly when I was pregnant with my first, and went back, popped more with the second, then retracted. With the third, I was in the labor room after three days of labor, still doing natural childbirth, but I was exhausted, my hair and pillow soaking wet, my lips cracked and bleeding from the breathing, lying on that paper sheet in a pile of moisture and blood, so much pressure from each contraction that it went all the way into my legs so that I had to keep my knees bent, yet so weak I had to rest them against each other in order to keep them raised, when the nurse came in. Apparently she noticed something strange, because she ran out to find the doctor who was on duty, and he was busy with someone else, so they wheeled me into the delivery room, put on the white leggings, strapped my wrists in. Just as a mask was placed over my face I saw the doctor enter the room. They performed a Caesarean just in time, as the uterine wall was about to burst. Since then, the vein's never gone away. If I ever got pregnant again, I'd get an abortion."

At the word *abortion* I witnessed thousands of drops of perspiration forming instantaneously on his face.

"What's wrong?" I asked, alarmed. He was spilling champagne all around.

"I'm chairman of the Committee to Repeal Abortion Laws," he said.

"Oh," I said, holding his drink for him. "Is your wife on the committee too?"

"She shows the movies about the horrors of abortion."

Joseph came over. "We're going to eat now." He gives us both a suspicious look. He's very insecure because of his impotence, but he's wrong to suspect me at every turn.

I pictured the old man and me together. We are

232

under a table, sheltered by the white tablecloth, which hangs down around us like a tent, enclosing only us and about twelve pairs of assorted shoes and legs. He pulls down his trousers to the tops of his thighs, his belly flaccidly flapping, white and speckled like a dead mackerel, his testicles hanging over the top of his pants, two small lumps in long, vulnerable scrotal sacs like poached eggs peering over toast.

"Don't get undressed," he whispers, "just take off your shoes." His freckled hand tremblingly cups his penis, pale and small as a toadstool in moss. As I kick off my shoes he stares at my feet with small, light blue watery eyes, and with his other hand gently traces the tendons on my metatarsal. "I have somethings to tell you," he says. "I'm impotent."

"Oh, that's okay," I say. He continues touching my feet, moving frantically from one to the other, and rubbing his penis with the other hand. Blood is rushing to his face, he's flushed, eyes bloodshot, but his penis is still tiny. He protects it with his hand as he strokes my foot, then, more and more excited, he begins stroking all the feet and shoes, male and female, Florsheim, Thom McCann, Kitty Kelly, that encircle us under the table. I hear them whispering above, "What's that?" "I thought it was you." "Feels like a dog." "What would a dog be doing here?" The tablecloth raises on one side, flooding us with light. A face peers under. The man is purple, he's writhing and gasping, still trying to touch shoes.

"What are you doing here?"

"He's trying to get some shade," I say, pointing to the man. "He doesn't feel well." I come out from under the table.

"I hope these facilitate some regeneration of the aging tissues of my brain," I said to Joseph, who was soaking up the sauce from the sweetbreads with Italian bread.

"What are these?" asked a woman, pointing to the

233

next course, already being served on that side of the table. She stuck her fork into her food tentatively.

"Those are Rocky Mountain Oysters."

"Yeah, bulls' balls," I said.

Another woman said, "Ohh, good," and she slit one across with the slow delectation of a Salvador Dali film.

"I don't like the idea of cutting off the balls of anything," one of the men said.

"The way men feel about balls, you'd think they were sacred. They identify with everything." Her husband took away her glass of champagne after she said that, but the woman grabbed it back. "Men are so afraid of being symbolically castrated because they do it to themselves," she said.

"I love these," said the woman next to me. "I have a great recipe for this."

"Wait a minute," I said. I wasn't that interested in food, but I thought if it was a good recipe I didn't want to miss it. I lfited my left breast and pushed it toward her face so that she could speak into the mike. She was startled when my nipple stared her in the eye, but she continued:

"This is for Rocky Mountain Oysters in Almond Velvet Sauce. Two tablespoons butter, two tablespoons flour, one-quarter teaspoon salt, one-eighth teaspoon pepper, and one cup of milk, for the sauce. Now, you take these Rocky Mountain Oysters in your hand gently, two per person, and immerse them in a pot with two quarts of boiling salted water for five minutes."

"Sssssss." One of the men sucked in his breath as if in pain.

"Then you braise them in a frying pan, in which some mushrooms and chopped onions have been cooking until golden brown, for another ten minutes, turning gently and adding some salt and pepper. Then you serve them with the white sauce, to which was added one cup of slivered almonds."

"Yum, yum."

"I like them with Bordelaise sauce. Listen to this celery," she said, biting of a piece and crunching it in my ear. "Yesterday I bought celery. All of it was wilted. I said, 'Take it back,' and the man delivered another one. Wilted. I told the delivery boy, for two dollars a bunch it shouldn't be wilted, and he said, 'Listen, lady, you have to take what you get. You're at the mercy of large corporations. Your money isn't power anymore.' "

"I belong to a food co-op," I said, "and we buy our own food at Hunt's Point wholesale market once a week, and divide it up. It's much less money and we buy fine, fresh stuff."

I picture these people in the food co-op. We're driving our small truck through the lanes of enormous trucks at Hunt's Point. I climb down from my seat, making sure my keys are still in my jeans pocket. Then our new member, Mrs. Bellows, lifts the hem of her black gown and slowly descends from the high step of the truck, trying not to twist her ankle on the gray tar-and-gravel road, balancing on one silver high heel until she's completely down.

"This is a terrible neighborhood," she says. "I don't know how people can live this way." Hal, our driver, jumps up the wooden platform about three feet above the level of the parking lot, where all the stalls are located, while I go look for the stairs. I see Mrs. Bellows attempting to get her foot up, then her knee, getting it caught with her gown under it, and trying to hoist her weight onto the platform, assisted from below and above by the men who cart the crates. Finally they swing her up, her gown ripping from top to bottom in front on a rough piece of wood. Attempting to recover her dignity while pretending to look at tomatoes, holding her dress together at the breasts and across her hips, she asks prices of the fruitmen, who stare at her, astounded, all their voyeuristic fantasies come true.

235

"How much are these tomatoes?" she asks, pointing to the crates.

"Six dollars, but you can have them for two."

"Thank you so much," says Mrs. Bellows, surprised. The men laugh. "But you have to go in the back with us."

"No, thank you. That's only a four-dollar profit. It doesn't make good business sense." Breasts flying, still holding her dress together, Mrs. Bellows has all the men working, carting the crates to our truck and opening them, while she directs. Once inside the truck, she removes her shoes, lets her dress fall off, and sorts the food with abandon, throwing apples and oranges into the bags, dipping her arms up to the elbows in chopped meat while ducking flying pears.

I hadn't noticed how much everyone was drinking. Some of the women were lying across the table. Joseph wanted to dance to Guy Lombardo's band, but I asked him to wait awhile so I could get some interviews. The woman next to me was staring into space, fiddling her spoon in some pudding. It was a perfect time to talk to her because there were no men around.

"Hi," I said. There was no answer. I put my hand on her and she fell over a bit. "Hello," I said, smiling. Tears ran down her cheeks.

"No one's been that friendly to me in a long time," she wept. "You touched me and smiled warmly. Oh, I'm so tired of talking about celery. I'm so lonely."

"But you're married," I said. "What's it like to be married to a corporation man?"

"To tell you the truth, it's horrible. I'm so lonely. Even at parties. And I never do anything right. There's always a special way to do things and I can never learn it. Even when I'm talking to one of our friends or to my husband, I feel an invisible wall of isolation, as if I can't reach anyone, as if I don't know who I am, and then I panic, I feel nauseous and terrified, I can't breathe, and I have to run out. Then I know there's

236

something wrong with our relationship. The few times that Bill shows me any affection, he's impotent. He says it's my fault because my breasts aren't shaped in a way that turns him on, which is slightly conical, and my nipples are the wrong shade. They're pinkish and he likes mauve."

I was tired of holding up my breast for her to speak into the mike, so I removed the tape recorder, first removing the mike, then digging my hand all the way into my waistband, down into my crotch, and pulled it out. She spoke with relish directly into the microphone.

"We always begin making love with an argument. Bill always wants me to wear a special costume of black tights and high heels and paint my nipples mauve and walk around the room in a very affected way, wiggling my hips. I always say that he doesn't really love me, just that routine, which has nothing to do with me, and he says that if I can't do it I don't love him. He always wins, and I walk around the room, while he says, 'Wiggle your hips . . . hold your breasts,' as he lies on the bed playing with himself. Then, when I see that his penis is slightly erect, I usually go over to him and lie down. That never fails to turn him off. His penis, still in his hand, becomes limper and disappears into his fist like ice cream leaking out the bottom of a cone. By this time I want to make love very badly, so I caress his penis with my hand, wrapping it around the way he does. He tells me exactly how to rub it, how to stroke it. He says, 'faster . . . slower, the whole thing . . . now the top.' I pump it up hopefully, I pump, pump, hold my breath. Then, like a tire with a leaky inner tube, it always deflates. At that moment I usually fall asleep from anguish, still holding on the way a baby holds a piece of her blanket."

"Is your husband impotent?" I asked someone else, holding my microphone under her chin.

"Only sometimes. Most of the time, after looking at some of his expensive books with sexual pictures, and some kissing and fellatio, usually he can stuff it in me like chopped meat into stuffed pepper, where, if it works, it's okay."

Before it was time to leave I danced a fox trot with Joseph.

"You sure create a lot of attention," he said.

"I'm sorry. I told you it might not be good for me to come. But everyone seems to like me."

"They just pretend. By tomorrow I could be quietly fired. Besides, they don't really like you, they just want to go to bed with you."

"What about the women? Do they want to go to bed with me?"

"Yes."

We were in a restaurant. Joseph was wiping up his gravy with bread and gobbling stuffed mushrooms.

"Listen, I'm having some important people for dinner, like the City Comptroller, the Mayor, the president of a ballistic-missile company . . . I'm not sure yet who, but I wonder whether you'd like to make the dinner because I know you like to cook. Just an informal dinner in my townhouse. You can cook anything you like."

I stared at him in wonderment! What an incredible suggestion! As soon as I was able to control the purple tremor of my face and retract my tongue and relax it enough to speak, I decided that instead of venting my anger at him now in the restaurant, ruining the rendezvous of his oral cavity with those succulent, oily mushrooms, residing on their heads in a bed of grease, and destroying the delectation of his dinner, I'd play an incredible joke on him.

He gave me the key to the townhouse to use while he was at work. I had all day to cook. It was going to be hard to keep Joseph out of the kitchen until the moment when I brought in the food. I knew he'd love to taste

238

it, smell it, see it, rub his thumbs in it. I could picture him lifting the cover, dipping his finger in, putting it to his nose, and then letting it fall into his mouth, which opens like the San Andreas fault during an earthquake, jowls waving as he nods, eyes contracting in ecstasy. I could put on my costume in the pantry, or I could cover it with an apron like the one my mother sent from Fort Lauderdale for Christmas, made by members of the Diabetic Association of America.

"Hi, honey. How are you doing?" Joseph came into the kitchen, looking for the pots.

"Joseph, I'm sorry, I know you want to peek, but I really want everything to be a surprise, so please go out and promise me you won't come in."

"Oooh, please, just let me see. What do you care? Besides, I'm starving."

"I do care, Joseph. Don't be childish."

My kids were running all over the kitchen, shouting and eating all the hors d'oeuvres. Timothy was slicing the collard-and-beet-green salad with his hands dripping streaks of playground dirt. I used the mirror on the back of the pantry door to put on my blackface. I dipped my hands into the can, which was like a can of black shoe polish, and patted it all over my face, like chocolate icing, except for my lips, which stood out brightly, appearing thicker than they were. My hair, very curly anyway, was put up in a dust rag. I was wearing a Hoover apron which had REMEMBER THE DEPRESSION silkscreened on it. I put the blackface all over my arms and hands, except for my palms. It was pretty messy and never seemed to dry completely. The kids wanted to wear it too, but I said they couldn't because it wasn't organic. Alex was making more peanut-butter hors d'oeuvres and I was cutting lemons for the punch. I was glad to be almost finished because I didn't enjoy cooking for large numbers of people. I peeked out of the kitchen and saw Joseph framed in the carved doorway to the living room like an early-

239

American painting, with a wooden smile. I watched him shake hands and make drinks for his guests for a moment, as they silently glided through the heavy carpet, soundless, like a sailing boat on a clean, windy day, in shiny shoes. The cut-crystal goblets and glasses of varying sizes, each correct for its drink, glittered with their golden contents and shot sparks of light into the air, reflecting from the multifaceted hanging parts of the crystal chandelier, which swung gently and heavily from the opening and closing of the vestibule door. The table, a world of mirrors in itself, all set earlier in the day by Joseph's maid with crystal dishes, goblets, silver and flowers, reflected everything multi-fragmented and, like a comet, scintillated with a dazzling illumination of its own.

I had to shut the door because my children were kicking each other and screaming. Before the door shut, through a tiny sliver I got a glimpse of Joseph's highly polished shoe, his knife-edge pleated-perfect slacks, and knew he was coming this way. As the door swung in, and before it stopped, he pulled it out forcefully, surely, and entered the kitchen. He glanced at me cursorily.

"I thought I paid you and gave you your carfare hours ago. You know I didn't need you tonight."

"How can you say you care for me when you can't even recognize me."

"Who is it? Who is it?" He wheeled around in surprise, belatedly recognizing my voice.

"It's me." He didn't have the courage to look at me directly out of both eyes, but stood sideways, like a cat approaching something to attack. "It's me," I said again.

"But . . . you're black. How could you do this? Do you know who's out there?"

"Who? A bunch of prejudiced people?"

Timothy was busy cutting beet greens again, the gray of his hands mingling with some red beet juice. Alex

240

and Zach, fighting on the floor, rolled over Joseph's shoe. Then he noticed them.

"What's this?" he said. "I hope they're going to stay in the kitchen. I invited eight people for a reason. Exactly eight is perfect for two four-way conversations."

"Well, then I have got to go out there or it'll destroy the balance."

"Do you know who's here? Do you know who's here?" he repeated again and again.

"Who?" I asked, out of passivity, feeling manipulated by the repetition of the question.

"Kleindienst, Rockefeller, Mayor Lindsay, Caspar Wainberger, Herman Badillo, and Mario Biaggi!"

"No women? If I go out there it will destroy the balance."

"It's okay for you to be a woman because you're cooking."

"Well, why didn't you ask Rockefeller to cook? Or Badillo to make *arroz con pollo*, or Biaggi to make an Italian dinner?"

"Look," he said, "you're getting hysterical. Why do you have to cause trouble? Can't you just be nice? It's almost time to bring out the hors d'oeuvres. Don't let the kids come out of the kitchen."

No wonder he's impotent, I thought, in blind anger, he's afraid he's going to do something wrong, I picture us in bed. He has prepared for it by finding time to study a new sex manual. We kiss and do foreplay. He does everything the manual specifies to excite me, including fondling and kissing my erogenous zones: a. lips; b. nipples; c. tongue in ear. Unable to recall with certainty about my navel, he gives it a quick feel and semiperforates it with an instant index finger, and eliminates cunnilingus as being too heady and a substitute for the real thing. I become excited only because it doesn't take much to get me excited. I press more and more closely until we're lying on our sides. He wonders what to do next. According to the book, I'm

241

not on my side at all. Where was he supposed to be that he wasn't, that caused me now to be on my side? And himself too. Perhaps he used the incorrect ratio of counterpressure. And I was sucking his nipples! The book didn't say anything about a woman sucking his nipples! He could begin again or push me into the position the book described on the pages he was trying tonight in the hopes of being more successful. He reorganized himself. Were all the factors coming into play? Olfactory? Tactile? Visual? He decides to push me onto my back, props my legs up, and throws a pillow under my ass. He seems to measure the distance between my two raised knees, and, slightly doubtful without immediate access to a compass and ruler, he studies me closely in the correctly dim light to ascertain whether I've broken out in the sex flush, those hivelike red blotches indicative of readiness. No blotches. But what were those marks on my face and neck? Were they merely from his beard? He feels my vagina to test the lubrication and, after a moment of indecision, decides that I'm ready. It isn't until then that he notices that he isn't.

I went to the worktable where the hors d'oeuvres were.

"You wait here," I said to the children. "You can come out later, but I need you to help in here." I screamed at Alex, who was rolling on the floor with Timothy. "Alex, Alex, Alex, Alex." She didn't hear. I lifted her up by her shirt. "Alex, finish the punch, cut these fruits in while I go in the other room. If you watch the boys I'll give you a quarter."

"If you give her a quarter you have to give me a quarter too," Timothy said.

"You have to give me a quarter too," said Zachary.

"Then you have to give me fifty cents," said Alex.

Zach looked up at me. "I want candy now."

"Well, I can't get it now."

"Then I'll ruin everything till I get it, Lynda."

242

"Then you wouldn't get it anyway. I can't reward you for naughtiness."

"Okay, Lynda. You'll see, Lynda." His face screwed up and his eyes looked at me through sudden tears like swollen seeds in a shallow stream, as I slipped out the door with the tray of hors d'oeuvres.

I stepped from the tile of the kitchen onto the parlor rug, so thick it almost threw me askew with my tray. No one even looked up as I approached, but Joseph began to sweat when he saw me. He came over and, as I put the tray on the table, introduced me. "This is Lynda Schor. I asked her to cook for us tonight." They nodded and resumed conversing as if I were semi-invisible. I recognized Lindsay and Rockefeller. Herman Badillo I had met in the A&P, and I recalled Biaggi from his photo in the *Villager* making a speech in support of the right to love whomever you want, for the Gay Activists Alliance. I picked up one of the hors d'oeuvres from the tray, a square, lightly covered with a soft caramelly topping which had leveled out and glossed over, giving it a soft vinyl appearance, like a stuffed plastic sculpture by Oldenburg. Joining the group (one two-way conversation of the two four-way conversations), I put the now-bent beige cube, pressed between my thumb and forefinger, into Herman Badillo's face.

"Have an hors d'oeuvre," I said.

"That's just what we were talking about. They look very exotic, but they taste somewhat like peanut butter. May I ask what's in them?"

"Peanut butter on white," I answered.

"How quaint."

"Do you support day care, Mr. Badillo?" I asked.

"Do you?" he asked suspiciously.

"I asked you first. What do you intend to do about day care if you're elected?"

"What's wrong with it?" he asked.

Caspar Weinberger came over. "This new program

243

of President Nixon's is totally revolutionary. It will do away with welfare and day care! Listen, it's a brainstorm. You use the day-care centers for the children of women on welfare. Then you send these women out to work at different jobs, filling up the work force, performing government jobs, clerical jobs, manual jobs, social-service jobs, their own welfare jobs, even taking care of their own kids in the day-care centers (they're always asking for parent boards and community control), at very low rates of pay, or just for their welfare checks, thereby helping in the President's austerity program. This way the day-care centers and welfare can be self-subsisting and self-supporting. The government and the taxpayers waste too much money on these things when they're mismanaged."

"What about the parents and mothers who can't afford private day care and are self-supporting now? Won't they have to go on welfare?" I asked.

"They always manage. I'm sure they'll manage. Or if they go on welfare, we'll just find them work in our program. That'll keep wages low. It will also keep the unions in line by supplying alternative laborers. The unions keep requesting enormous raises. With plenty of people available accepting low wages for the same union jobs, we'll be more able to negotiate. The union leaders agree with this administration. After all, they have everything to gain if they go along with us instead of the worker. We offer them incentives." He winked. "We can't allow our economy to fold." Caspar Weinberger bites into an hors d'oeuvre and his mouth sticks together. "Hey, Biaggi, am I right?" he mumbles. "Listen," says Caspar, "I have an even more revolutionary idea, that I must admit was given to me by Richard Nixon, but I've elaborated on it quite a bit and soon I'm sure we'll get it passed by Congress. In my opinion, it's even good enough to bypass Congress."

"Listen, Caspar," interrupts Lindsay, "if you want to talk, don't eat any of these," and he rips a peanut-butter square from the hand of Weinberger. Mario

Biaggi has one hand piled high with the peanut-butter squares and is wiping some, with his other hand, off his dark pin-stripe suit.

"Great idea," he says, waving his hand. "These remind me of my childhood. Makes me nostalgic."

"They don't make me feel nostalgic," said Rocky. "Caviar would. From the Black Sea. Umm. Or the Caspian Sea, reddish, like strawberry jelly."

"I could never get used to that salt taste," said Biaggi.

"I don't want to remember my childhood," said Weinberger. "The nuclear family is breaking up, and it's the thing that holds America together. That's where this excellent new plan comes in," he said. "If we can bring back the nuclear family, we can end day care *and* welfare, and we can do this by using the day-care centers as marriage bureaus with marriage brokers and social halls. A woman on welfare will have to go there to meet a man or else have her stipend rescinded. Every effort would be made to find good mates, do expert matchmaking, and no one will have to pay a fee, except maybe the man. Maybe we could use some of the profits, aside from more protective military spending and paying off municipal bonds to the banks, for a computer, for real computerized matchmaking. What do you think?"

"I'm astounded," I said.

"Watch what you're telling," Kleindienst said. "Do you know who she really is? No. Maybe she's a member of the Black Panthers. Have you checked up on her? Maybe she's a revolutionary."

"She's my friend," said Joseph.

"Do you really know who she is? You can never even be sure who your wife or lover is," said Kleindienst. "I'm only kidding," he added, looking at Joseph's hurt face, "but there's a little bit of truth in every joke."

"Ha, ha, you are so profound. Why doesn't everyone sit down?"

"Yeah," said Lindsay. "I'm in agreement with that."

245

"Honey," Joseph said to me, touching my waist where the Hoover apron strings were bunched under the regular apron strings lumping up, "let's have some of that food."

In the kitchen the kids were eating. I put on my waitress cap, a little lacy thing that sat on top of my head, and a lace apron.

"Is the punch ready?" I asked Alex, who was eating from the salad bowl with her fingers, licking the dressing off them and returning them to the bowl to forage for more stuff, picking around with two fingers for the pieces she wanted. Clad in tights with brightly colored flowers winding up and down her legs, and her gaudily colored shorts and shirt, her black straight hair hanging down her back except for the four thin braids in the front, banded with yellow and red rubber bands, her own, which she keeps in her room with her other rubber bands, for which she has a fetish, she looked somewhat like an Indian.

I looked for the punch. My favorite recipe: white wine, apple juice, a bit of fresh squeezed orange juice, all kinds of fresh fruit squeezed in and sliced on, cloves, and cinnamon sticks. Tonight I had substituted Thunderbird for the white wine. I studied its ocher tones, made deeper by the Thunderbird, and noticed how so much of what I was serving was yellow ocher. The fruit floated on top. Alex had done a good job except that it was riddled with orange and grapefruit pits, which floated about with the cloves and rode atop the slices of fruit. I'd never have time to pick out all those pits.

"Did you have to leave these pits in?" I asked Alex.

"It's too hard to pick all the pits out of the fruit. They can always spit them out," she said. "You complain about all your work, why don't you make things simpler like I do?" she asked.

"You're right," I said.

246

I carried out the large heavy punch bowl, both arms around it like an infant carrying a basketball, my gum platform soles getting stuck in the carpet, and finally was able to place it on the table where everyone was seated, without breaking any of the mirrors as I put it down. I proceeded to serve it with the sterling ladle into the cut-glass wineglasses.

"Don't we have any wine?" asked Joseph.

"I thought I'd make this punch instead. It's more interesting and suits the meal better." I poured it into the glasses, dripping fruit and wine on the table. Joseph was twitching.

"Why isn't the table set with a cloth?" he asked.

"I took it off because I didn't want it to get dirty," I told him.

"What do you call this amazing creation?" asked Biaggi. They all looked at me, as if the question were worthy of an inspiring answer.

"I call it Public Assistance Punch."

"Fantastic! What a clever name!"

"Of course," I said, "true Public Assistance Punch has many variations. It can be made with only juice and fruit, or just juice. Or just gin and pits, or Thunderbird and rinds, or just beer." I noticed Timo standing next to Joseph and Rockefeller, near the head of the table.

"Quiet," said Rockefeller. "This little fellow's going to recite a haiku." Timo stood there with a strangely determinedly shy poise, his slightly Oriental eyes coarctated in concentration.

> "Bubble gum, juicy chewy
> I ask to buy some.
> 'D'you think I'm made of money?' "

As everyone clapped, I watched Timothy pass his Army fatigue cap his father got him for coins. At that moment Alex entered, carrying something in a dirty dishtowel, Zachary leaking out behind her, into the dining room from the kitchen like bacteria into a sterile test tube. Alex noticed Timothy, who was showing Zachary his money, and tried to kick them back inside because she didn't want to jeopardize her fifty cents. Since her hands were full, she kicked her patterned-tight–clad legs behind her at the mesmerized boys, the dish in the towel shaking precariously.

"Get back in," she said. "Don't bug me."

Suddenly Kleindienst rose from the table in a panic. "Bug, who said bug? Who said, 'Don't bug me'? What do you mean?"

"Sit down."

"Someone get him a drink."

I gave him a sip of Thunderbird and he rose like half-baked cupcake mix.

"What's that?" he shouted as soon as his throat stopped contracting. The kids were standing in a row, watching as if they were in Radio City viewing *Mary Poppins.*

"I told you before about the kids," hissed Joseph. "I never thought you'd bring them!"

"I can't help it," I said, "I'm on welfare and I have no money for baby-sitters."

"Oh, no, how could you tell that right in front of my friends," wept Joseph.

"It's okay, it's okay," Lindsay comforted, wrapping his arms around him. "I learned how to do this physical-contact stuff in sensitivity training and encounter groups at hotels," he said, explaining his gesture. "You know that joke, 'Some of my best friends are——' " He grinned winningly.

Caspar Weinberger asked me, suddenly inspired, "Are you getting paid for tonight?"

"I don't know, I may get paid later, or in the morning." I winked, pretending to be lascivious.

"Do you indulge in prostitution?" he asked in a crafty way.

I said, "How else can I live with three kids on welfare, with the inflation index rising every day?"

248

"Prostitution is illegal."

"No, there's a new liberalized law," said Lindsay, restraining him, "allowing prostitutes not to be arrested unless they're caught soliciting."

"Well, we'll have to do something about that," said Rockefeller.

"Are you getting paid for tonight?" Weinberger asked again.

"Of course not, I'm just helping Joseph," I said.

"If you were, we'd have to investigate your case. You're not allowed to earn any extra income, you know. What's your case number?" he asked, preparing to write it on his napkin.

"Hey, you can't do that," said Joseph. "It's not a paper napkin."

"Oh, I'm sorry."

"She's not getting paid anyway," he said.

"I never get paid for what I do," I said proudly. "I always work for nothing."

"Right," said Joseph.

"Where's your husband?" asked Rockefeller. "You have to find him and sue him for child support. Remember the time when we used to make surprise investigations at night? We should bring that back. Those were the days. If we ever discovered you with Joseph we'd make him pay."

"Like hell," said Joseph.

Alex ventured to advance anew, still carrying her towel-wrapped contribution.

"I have a philosophy," said Badillo. "There are those who do plenty for nothing, and those who do nothing for plenty."

He'd barely finished, when Alex, progressing with her fur clogs across the carpet, dropped the dish, which, the moment the dishtowel hit the carpet, opened like a ripe flower, petals spewing off, and all over the carpet slack yellow-ocher pullulated.

"Oh my god, oh my god," screamed Joseph. "Oh my god."

249

"What's that?" asked Lindsay, getting up from his seat.

Biaggi came over and began probing it with a knife like someone inspecting dog shit to see whether his animal had worms.

"It was quiche Lorraine."

"Quiche Lorraine? I never saw quiche Lorraine like that, that color or consistency."

"I never saw quiche Lorraine on my rug before," said Joseph.

"This is quiche Lorraine made with peanut butter and white-bread croutons. It's a specialty in my *Welfare and Food Stamp Cookbook* I'm writing and compiling. Almost everything in it is made with peanut butter."

Alex stood there silently.

"What do you say, young lady," asked Joseph.

Alex just stood there.

"She doesn't speak to people," I said. "She can talk, but in certain situations she won't speak."

"Is she . . . ill?" he asked, tapping his head.

"Oh no, she just doesn't want to speak in certain types of situations."

"If you vote for me I can help you get her into Willowbrook," said Biaggi.

"Willowbrook . . ." I said in amazement. "But she's not retarded. Besides, I heard about Willowbrook. The kids are treated horribly there."

"Not so bad. After all, the kids are a mess. They don't know what's happening to them anyway. But they have a special group of kids they use for show— for the press and visitors—and I could get your daughter in that group. They keep those pretty neat, treat them well, even try to teach them . . . but she would have to be part of a hepatitis program."

"Hepatitis program?"

"Willowbrook is working in conjunction with a hepatitis program attempting to perfect the vaccine for hepatitis. The children in that group are given

the various vaccines they develop to see what happens."
He paused awhile. "You have to do something about
her. She won't become a useful member of society."
Then he thought for a moment. "Well, I guess it
doesn't matter much since she's a girl. All she has to
be able to do is take care of a house and kids. I once
read somewhere that retarded women make the best
wives. They're happier, work well, don't think about
things they can't do, don't want what they don't have,
enjoy housework, and are very loving."

"But they're funny-looking," said Lindsay.

"Why didn't you folks marry retarded women?" I
asked them as we stood around the ocher pile on the
green rug.

"I was too stupid. I wish I did, I wouldn't have all
this trouble with my wife," laughed Badillo.

Kleindienst looks at me slyly. He studies my outfit
and my black cheeks and hands, my serving tray.
"Our wives are not liberated like you."

Joseph laughs triumphantly.

Alex and I mopped up the peanut-butter–quiche pile
with endless paper towels and drippy trips into the
kitchen.

I took the chitterlings and hog maws in peanut-butter
sauce off the stove. Just in time. There were tiny dots
of splashed orange all over the stove and walls because the flame had been too high. Luckily, I wasn't
supposed to clean. I'd speak to his maid about the
new union of household workers, called Household
Technicians of Greater New York. The beet-green-
and-collard-green salad was ready. I needed the kids
to help me carry out these main dishes. Zachary had
found pretzels and potato chips and was lying down
on the floor eating them in the hypnotic state before
sleep. I didn't want to disturb him. Timothy was nowhere to be found. I asked Alex to carry out the sweet-
potato pie. The black-eyed peas were as hard as pebbles
because I couldn't decide whether I wanted to use

251

them until it was too late. Now I couldn't decide whether to serve them. I couldn't find the serving dishes, so I decided to bring the stuff out in the pots. In the dining room the air was filled with smoke, but a relief after chitterling air. Then I saw through the haze where Timo was. He was using his shoeshine kit, shining everyone's shoes. Just completing Mayor Lindsay's black shoes, he stood up with his hand out, collecting his money.

As we put the food on the table Badillo was saying, "But I didn't want them to build a housing project near my house. I'm all for low-cost housing, but not near me. Those people are dirty, they throw garbage all over, they sing and talk loud, they mug people, they take drugs—you can't bring them into better sections. So I had to fight the building of low-cost housing in my neighborhood. But it has nothing to do with not being interested in the interests and problems of the poor and minority groups. I haven't forgotten that I'm a minority group. I intend to do a lot for the Puerto Rican people. I'm going to propose that Fourteenth Street be extended all the way to Twenty-third Street."

"Well, I'll tell you one thing," said Rockefeller. "There won't be any drugs anymore when I get finished. Just people who make money selling them. Listen, I'm a powerful man. Ask Happy." There were childish snickers. "Over three thousand pages of testimony were taken in two months of hearings before the Codes Committee of the State Legislature, stating thousands of ways liberalized drug programs and attitudes helped alleviate the drug problem, and I ignored all of it, even though I had decided to appear personally before the hearing, which I never do. I was able to bargain for my tough drug laws by giving more needed judges, friends of mine who needed jobs. Next to money, bargaining is everything. Last week I signed my Drug Bills, the toughest antidrug program in the nation. I won out over the strange alliance of vested Establishment interests, political soft-liners such as the Judicial Conference, the District Attorneys Association, and New York City police officials, and others who joined forces and tried unsuccessfully to stop my program. I ignored all the stuff laid on me to break me down, protests of kids on campuses, business people. I ignored everything and came to my own conclusions. That's how I stay strong."

"Speaking of bills," said Kleindienst, "there's one I really wanted but it's still being considered, called the Bug Everyone Bill. Assemblyman John LoPresto wants it. It would enforce any person to assist the police in the placing of taps or other electronic surveillance anywhere. The bill not only applies to telephone-company employees and landlords, but could also, on court order, require wives to spy on husbands and parents to bug their children."

Joseph, in the meantime, was helping everyone to dinner.

"Hey, let's not talk shop," he said.

"This salad is fantastic," said Biaggi. "So inventive. I've never seen anything that's in here. I'm glad you didn't use plain old iceberg lettuce. I, for one, am observing the boycott."

Joseph was sweating. "I thought we weren't going to talk shop," he said.

I knew he was nervous because he had six iceberg lettuces in the hydrator of his refrigerator for me to use for salad.

"Listen, I'm for the farm workers too," said Lindsay, "but things are being done for them. For instance, a bill was passed stating that the farm owners have to provide water for migrant farm workers."

"Good, good," said Badillo.

"I don't exactly approve," said Weinberger. "They should get their own water, but I can see giving in a little. Don't forget, we made it on our own, they could too if we weren't too easy on them. When you give people too much they never learn to stand on their own two feet. This is the attitude that's already made America great."

"What's this?" asked Lindsay, pressing the sweet-potato pie. "It tastes like peanut butter."

"I don't want to question John's sense of reality, but it tastes like peanut butter to me too," said Joseph.

"It's sweet-potato pie made with peanut butter instead of sweet potatoes. It's also one of the recipes in my welfare cookbook."

"You encourage welfare by doing these things," said Weinberger. "It doesn't look good for our country to have people on welfare, and it's no good for the budget. In our country the right of the people is to help themselves."

I sat in the kitchen too miserable and exhausted to move. I'd planned to sneak out because I didn't think I'd like to face Joseph right away, but I decided not to. Zach was asleep with a potato chip sticking out of his mouth like a pacifier, causing cavities by the second; Timo was running around wildly and senselessly with exhaustion, and Alex was crying. I couldn't move, but just sat there listening to the guests leaving, with relief. Joseph came in.

"What a mess," he said, looking around the kitchen.

"Tough," I said. "I suppose you're livid with anger, but I wanted to play a joke on you for asking me to cook dinner for your friends."

"Oh, I'm not angry. They loved it. They said they never had such a good time. John Lindsay told me to ask whether you'd do the same thing at his house for one of his important dinners. And with your kids, too! He wants to know, since you don't belong to Actors Equity, if you'd give him a special rate."